# FINDING SOLACE

## KINGS OF RETRIBUTION MC

CRYSTAL DANIELS

SANDY ALVAREZ

# SANDY ALVAREZ
# CRYSTAL DANIELS

*Two Pens One Story*

*FOR OUR BROTHER*
*WE MISS YOU*

# 1

## REID

R oad Captain. That's my title—my position in The Kings of Retribution MC. It may sound egotistical of me, but I'm fuckin' good at what I do. As the Road Captain, I manage all the runs. I earned the position because I'm efficient at researching, planning, and organizing, right down to the tiniest of details for things to run as smooth as possible. If something goes wrong on the road, it's on me. My brothers trust in my ability to stay on top of things and plan accordingly because everything can change at a moment's notice. I have their backs as much as they have mine. Amongst other things, I'm good with a gun. Doc taught me and my little brother Noah alongside Logan growing up. My Pops, he taught me how to ghost out—not be seen. Over time it proved a valuable skill.

Am I a saint? Far from it. Have I taken someone's life? I've done things in my life for my club—for my family that would be considered ruthless and would do them again if it meant the end result kept them safe. Which is why my head is so fucked up. I've been laid up in this damn hospital and can't perform my responsibilities for my club. It's killin' me.

I thought losing my leg a few years ago was some of the toughest shit I had to try and overcome, but this...lying here in this shitty ass hospital bed all busted up with some loss of mobility to the lower half of my body because of swelling around my lower spine and my arm broken in two places is proving to be worse.

Waking up after the accident, I remember my first initial thoughts being of Alba and Leyna. Were they safe? Did Gabriel get to them in time? Eventually, everyone assured me both women were fine, and Alba and Gabriel had even welcomed their first child, but it didn't do much in ridding me of the guilt I felt that they were in danger in the first place. If I hadn't fallen asleep, I would have been there sooner, and none of it would have happened. Not only that, I couldn't believe I missed out on one of my brothers becoming a dad.

I'm starting to get sensation back in my legs, but not nearly enough to stand on my own. It's been four weeks of lying in this bed, and it's starting to wear on my nerves. Day in and day out, I lay here as people come in and out, poking and prodding me. Everyone tells me it will get better in time. Meanwhile, their lives are carrying on while mine is at a standstill. Sure, the guys have been coming in almost every day to catch me up on club shit, but it's done nothing to help my mood. The fact that I can't get up and walk on my own free will is fuckin' up my head way more than it should for someone who has already had to learn to walk twice in their life. Now I'm going to have to do it all over again.

A light knock on the door draws my attention away from the self-pity I'm rolling in. My nurse from the past few weeks, Vanessa, walks in wearing a smile on her face. "Good morning, Mr. Carter, it's time to work some more on you learning how to transfer yourself from the bed to your wheelchair before you get released today," she says.

Throwing my blanket to the side, I use my left arm and reach up for the support above my head and pull myself into an upright position, and attempt to move my lower half to the side of the bed. The nurse rolls my chair over, and I lower the bed.

"Okay, slowly shift your weight until you slide into the chair."

I'll have a better chair waiting for me at home, one I should be capable of handling on my own. It will be easier to use with my broken arm. I've gone from riding a 1973 Harley Davidson Shovelhead to a wheelchair. Frustration is getting the better of me, mostly because this damn cast hinders my ability to do more on my own, so I'm pretty much relying solely on my left arm to support the weight of my six-foot-two-inch frame. With a little assistance, I clear the bed and get my ass situated in the seat.

"Great, let's do this a few more times before the doctor makes his rounds this morning," she encourages me.

I have to give her a lot of credit. My nurse has put up with my moody ass for weeks. Even when I've gotten to the point I've wanted to punch myself for being such a dick.

"You know...I'm gonna miss seeing all those handsome men coming through here every day to visit you. It gives all us nurses something to look forward to," she playfully says with a smile as she stands close by in case I need her to assist me.

"I'm ready to get the hell out of here," I grunt as I finish hoisting myself across the edge of the hospital bed and into the wheelchair.

"You should be starting a more vigorous form of physical therapy soon. Don't worry, before you know it; you'll be on your feet again," she tells me.

We do this several more times for an hour until my muscles are on fire from the workout I've given them. In all, I only needed assistance one time. Vanessa helps me back into the bed before saying her goodbyes. "I have faith that in a couple of months you'll be walking. Stay positive," she says before walking out the door.

I'm closing my laptop after checking on the delivery status of the equipment I ordered a week ago when I hear someone rap on my door, and Prez comes strolling in.

"Hey, Prez, what brings you here this morning?" I ask. "I thought you and the guys had a meeting with the city council about the new building going up downtown."

"Still do. I just wanted to swing by and see if there is anything the brothers and I can do to help get things ready for you to go home," he states as he strides over to the chair across the room by the window and takes a seat.

I feel terrible that he has so much on his plate. Jake has taken over running the construction company with Nikolai while I'm laid up. Our company is brand new and is doing well. I know Jake is more than qualified to help keep things running, but hopefully, that will all change just as soon as I get settled into a new routine at home.

"Yeah, I have a guy delivering some equipment sometime today. Maybe have one of them hang out at my place for a while just in case I don't get out of here in time."

"Sure, they going to install this stuff too?" he asks.

"Yeah," I inform him. "And I'm sorry all this shit has been put on your shoulders, Prez."

"It's nothin' I can't handle. Logan has taken full control of the daily running of the shop, and Quinn hired another mechanic to help. We got it all covered, son."

"A repairman is supposed to swing by my place around noon to fix the old freight elevator in the back that I never got around to working on. I'll need to make sure it's up and running before I get home, or I'll be sleeping on the couch in my office," I tell him.

Leaning forward, Prez looks at me. "Listen, I know this may have been mentioned to you by the doctor already, but have you thought about hiring home care while you're still recovering? Don't go taking all this shit on by yourself. I know you, Reid."

Of course, the doctor made mention of it. At the time, I was against it, and I still am. The thought of having to rely on someone else to take care of me and my needs when I'm a grown-ass man doesn't sit well with me. Having to have help showering, getting dressed, or even using the damn bathroom is not easy for me. The last thing I need is a lecture. I know it's coming from a good place, but at the moment I don't want to hear it.

Clearing his voice, Prez stands up from his chair. "If help is what the doctor thinks you need then you should do it. Pride can be a man's downfall. Do whatever it takes to get better," he says in a firm, fatherly voice. It makes me think of my old man and the fact that if he were still alive, he would be kicking my ass right now for feeling angry and sorry for myself.

"I'll give it some more thought," I tell Jake.

"I've got to run. I'll send Quinn over to your place later, and I'll have Nikolai email the contracts for your final approval this evening. Think about what I said," he informs me before walking out the door, closing it behind him.

I'm not sure how to deal with feeling useless or feeling like I don't know where I fit in with my club anymore. I was born into the lifestyle. Hell, I knew as soon as I turned eighteen, I was going to prospect with the MC. The fact that my old man was a founding member held no bearing. The club members treated me like any other prospect. It helped shape me into who I am today, and now I feel like an outsider looking in. What if I'm never able to ride again? All the 'what ifs' are weighing me down.

And what about my personal life? Not to say I don't get my needs met. But what if I never walk again? It was hard enough dealing with the fears of rejection or judgment after the loss of my right leg, and now I can't use either one.

There is a knock on the door, followed by Dr. Brown, my neurologist walking into the room, "Mr. Carter, are you ready to leave us today?" he asks.

"Yeah, Doc. I've been fuckin' ready. When are you letting me out of here?"

"The nurse is getting your discharge papers ready now." He looks down at his watch then looks back up. "I would say you'll be good to go in about thirty minutes. You have someone to take you home?"

"I do," I tell him.

"First, we need to go over a few things. You'll be starting physical therapy the day after tomorrow at our facility across the street, and you'll be going at least two to three times a week. You'll also follow up with me once a week. I'm not 100% convinced you are going to be able to handle things on your own. You may require professional help, so I sent your chart over to InCare Healthcare to get you set up with someone who can come out every day and get you to and from your appointments. Plus, help with other physical activities you are sure to need assistance with. At least until you get that cast off in four more weeks," he rambles off.

What the fuck gave him the impression he could go and make that decision for me? I take a couple of deep breaths, calming my nerves. "I haven't decided on an in-home nurse." I scowl at him.

My phone ringing stops my rant from going any further. Reaching over, I grab it from the tray table on the left side of the bed and swipe the screen to answer, "What," I bark into the phone.

"How's it going, brother?" Quinn's voice says.

"Glad you called, man. Where are you at right now? Can you grab a ride and get my ass? They're letting me out of here in about twenty-five minutes."

"Prez ordered me to your place, so I was about to hop on my bike and ride over there."

The doctor looks at me, annoyance spreading across his face as he looks at his watch again. Fuck him. I've sat here all morning waiting for his ass to get in here. A few minutes of him waiting ain't gonna kill him.

"Assuming you're leaving now from the garage, you can grab my keys from Logan and go to my place and get my truck," I tell him.

"You got it. See ya soon."

Disconnecting the call, I toss my phone onto the bed, ready to continue the chat the doctor was having with me. Not bothering to apologize for the interruption, I cross my arms over my chest and look at him, waiting for him to continue. He shouldn't have taken the liberty of sending my file to InCare without my go ahead. I've made sure I'm more than prepared to go home. Not being able to walk doesn't make me an invalid.

"Mr. Carter, I'm aware that you are reluctant to receive help, but believe me when I say you'll be grateful for it. Therapy alone will wear you out physically and mentally. You'll need someone around that's capable of taking care of you."

"I'll make that decision for myself," I clip.

Sighing, he flips through the papers on his clipboard and hands them to me, "Here's a prescription for the muscle relaxers you've been taking and some mild pain medication as well. The second form is your appointment for later this week and the number to InCare. If you're not willing to accept the help, then give them a call and cancel everything. Get home and give it some thought beforehand. You might change your mind, Mr. Carter." He shakes my hand. "I'll see you in a week," he adds before leaving my room.

It doesn't take long before Quinn comes walking in with a duffle bag in his hand, "Didn't know what all you had here to put on, so I grabbed you some gym clothes out of your closet."

It looks like I'm not the only one in a foul mood. "Appreciate it, brother. What's eating you?" I ask.

He runs his hand through his shaggy blond hair and lets out a heavy sigh, "Ran into Dr. Evans, on my way up here. That woman. All I'm trying to do is be nice, but she insists on trying to cut off my balls every time I speak to her. I don't get it. I'm a likable guy." He throws his hands up.

Yeah, Quinn's idea of being friendly doesn't stop at a hello, especially when it comes to women. "You ever stop to think she doesn't like your endless flirting and pet names all the time? Maybe try and have an actual conversation with her instead of letting your dick control your mouth." I laugh.

Grabbing the bag, I pull out the clothes he brought. As I'm slipping on the shirt, he responds. "My mind goes blank when I see her, man. Flirting comes naturally to me. Normally it works."

"Yeah, it works when the woman is looking for nothing but a good time. Emerson doesn't strike me as the type to want to have fun," I tell him. I recognize it because I'm the same way. Driven. After I've gotten some socks on, I start the task of putting on my sweatpants with Quinn watching me struggle.

"You need help, man?" he asks me.

"No, I got it." It takes a few minutes to work them up to my thighs before I stop and look at Quinn, who's still looking at me.

"Do you have to stare, brother?"

"Sorry." He turns his back to me, "I can help. I mean, as long as you can keep your dick from slapping me in the face, I can help you get your clothes on." He puts his hands in his pockets and rocks back on the heels of his feet.

I know Quinn wants to help, but this is different, I'm a grown-ass man. A few more attempts and I manage to get them the rest of the way then slip my shoes onto my feet. "I don't mean to be such a dick. I'm trying to do this on my own. Except for these shoes." I point down my feet. "I can't tie the fuckers with one hand."

He walks over and kneels, "No judgment from me, Reid. If you ever need help, you ask. It goes no further than us. I won't say shit to no one."

"Thanks. Give me a minute to slide my ass into this wheelchair, and we can go."

A few minutes later, I've got my shit packed, and I'm rolling out the door with a nurse accompanying me down to the waiting truck that Quinn just parked. That's when I realize there is no way I'm going to be able to lift myself into the cab of the truck.

"I'm going to have to lift you into the truck, brother. You good with that?" Quinn asks.

Time to suck it up, as my old man would tell me. Suddenly, the full picture of just how hard it will be during my recovery hits me, "Do what you gotta do, man. It looks like I'll be finding other means of transportation for a while. Something that sits low enough that I can get in and out of on my own," I tell him. Once I position my chair as close as I can get it to the opening of the truck door, I let Quinn lift me into the cab. He doesn't say a word, which I'm grateful for.

Sighing, I reach across and buckle my seat belt. I guess I'll be keeping that arrangement for home care after all.

---

WE FINALLY PULL up to my home. It's an old, historic two-story firehouse I converted into a two-bedroom loft apartment a few years ago. Quinn stuck around long enough to help make sure the guys that delivered the medical equipment got everything set up. Now that the repairman has the lift working, I wheel myself onto it and push the button taking myself to the upstairs floor to inspect everything.

"Hey, man, if you have it from here, I'm gonna get going. Logan needs me to close up the shop later, and I need to finish the oil change and tune-up on a bike before morning," Quinn says as he comes walking from the kitchen area with a sandwich in his hand.

"Yeah, I got it from here," I tell him as I make my way out of the

CRYSTAL DANIELS & SANDY ALVAREZ

elevator. It's a little creaky as the gears kick in, but not bad, considering they are part of the original system.

On the ride home, I gave in and called InCare to discuss my options and what I would require along the way for recovery. They suggested the best route to go would be 24-hr assistance, which means whoever they send would need a room to stay in for at least the next four weeks until I get this damn cast off my arm.

The last time I shared space with someone was with my brother when we were kids. I have problems trusting people and even bigger issues trusting a woman. I prefer being on my own. Having things precisely the way I like them—my way.

Quinn takes a bite from the sandwich he's holding in his hand and immediately turns, spitting it into the kitchen sink. "What the fuck, man? This tastes like ass."

"Yeah, I bet it does. That shit's been in there for a month now. Your ass should have checked it first, shithead." I laugh at him and watch as he walks over to the trash can and chunks the rotten food inside.

"You need some groceries, man. Why don't you call Bella and have her load you up?" he says.

"I'll deal with it," I tell him.

"Alright. Call me if you need anything, brother, and let me know how things go in the morning. Seriously, I'm glad you decided to give the home care a try for the next few weeks."

"Yeah, well, I'm not promising anything. I'll see how it goes. I'll see ya tomorrow, Quinn," I tell him as he waves and walks out the door.

Not having someone push me around is refreshing, and it is much easier to maneuver around my place. The layout of my upstairs is an open concept. On one side is my kitchen and dining room area. The other side is a relatively large living room complete with the original wood burning fireplace.

I make my way toward the back, down the hall. At first, all this space was once separated into smaller-sized rooms, big enough to fit bunk beds into. I made sure to preserve as much of the original brick that I could throughout the remodeling process. Keeping the industrial look and feel of the firehouse was important to me. I had the walls torn down and turned two of those bedrooms into a spare bedroom, and the others at the very end of the hall became my master. It's not oversized or extravagant, but it's enough for me.

I wheel over to my king size bed. The trapeze lift I ordered to help myself get in and out of bed looks to have been installed correctly. I wouldn't have bothered with it, but with the use of just one arm, I felt it would come in handy. Turning, I head to the bathroom and find they've done an excellent job installing the extra handrails in my walk-in shower. It already has a built-in bench that I hope to have no problems getting myself on and off of.

Going back to the kitchen, I rummage through the cabinets only to find a couple of boxes of macaroni and cheese, so I pull a pot out of the bottom cabinet and fill it with water before setting it on the stovetop to boil. I'm not the best cook. I usually get something to eat at the clubhouse or order takeout from somewhere. Once I have my dinner fixed, I decide to take it downstairs to my office. The lower level hasn't been finished yet. The only renovations I've done are put up some walls to give me office space. The rest of the area, I'm not sure what I want to do with it yet.

Opening the door, I flip the light switch. If I had to describe my office, I would say it looks like something out of the TV show *CSI*. Several flat screen computer monitors cover the entire wall in front of me and my desk, which has two desktop computers sitting on top. Yes, I'm a computer geek. Always have been. Sure, I love the club, my bike, my brothers, and doing construction jobs on the side, but this is my obsession. Ever since I can remember, besides wanting to be a club member, is being fascinated with technology and criminology. If it's been written, I've read it when it comes to those two subjects. I don't hold a degree in any of it, but my skills have helped the club in more ways than one. Hell, even local law enforcement calls me on occasions to help. On a freelance basis, that is. Let's say my skills have helped make me money over the years.

After spending a few hours down here, I turn everything off and head upstairs to bed. My first night alone, with no one coming in to bother me. Getting myself ready was relatively easy, and pulling myself from the chair to the bed was not so bad either. As I settle in for the night, I try to get myself into the right frame of mind and ready for the following days to come.

# 2

---

# MILA

"Good morning Mila," Brittany, a fellow nurse, greets me as she walks up to the nurse's station.

"Morning Brit," I respond with a smile while placing my purse on the counter. Looking at the clock on the wall, I notice I have ten minutes before my shift starts. "I'm going to run down to the cafeteria for some coffee. You want me to bring you back anything?"

"No thanks, I'm good." Brittany picks up her chart and turns to walk away. Abruptly stopping in her tracks, she whips around and snaps her fingers. "Shoot, I almost forgot. Kate wants to see you. She said to come to her office before starting your shift."

Kate is our supervisor. She's a 56-year-old mother of five. I couldn't ask for a better boss. She understands the challenges of having kids. Anytime one of us needs to leave early or take a day off to deal with our families, she is more than understanding.

I've wanted to be a nurse for as long as I can remember. My grandmother was a nurse. I remember watching the joy she had in taking care of others. I knew from a young age what my grandmother did was important, and she made a difference in people's lives.

That's what I wanted to do—make a difference. My parents couldn't disagree more, though. In their eyes, what I chose to do with my life is menial. To say I'm a disappointment to them is an understatement. I was supposed to go to Harvard and follow in my parent's footsteps, or at the very least, become a trophy wife. Being at your husband's beck and call and having Botox lunch dates with the wives of fellow firm partners is not my idea of a life.

My parents used to ship me off to my grandmother's every summer growing up. As soon as school was out, they put me on a plane to Montana. They didn't want to deal with having their child around. God forbid they spend time with their daughter. Every single summer that I can remember was spent with Grams. Then my parents were shocked when I turned out to be so much like her. If it weren't for my grandmother being in my life, I would have never known what it was like to be loved. My parents believed children should be seen and not heard. My grandmother believed children were gifts from God and should be cherished. The way my Grams loved me growing up has shown me how to be the mother I am today. My daughter Ava is everything to me, and I always make sure to show her how much she is loved. I never once thought a one-night stand would change my life forever.

When I found out at nineteen that I was pregnant, my parents said I had two options: abortion or adoption. I chose adoption. Only, in the end, I couldn't go through with it. My parents went to great lengths to hide me and my pregnancy. I was to have my baby, hand her over to the adoptive parents, and then simply move on with the life they had mapped out for me as if nothing ever happened. I was in the hospital, hours away from having my baby girl when the adoption papers were shoved in my face. I stared down at those papers for an hour. My shaky hand held a pen to the signature line. I knew in my heart I would regret for the rest of my life the decision to give up my daughter. She was a part of me, and I was already in love with her. My mother noticed my hesitation and told me, "Sign those papers, or you'll be on your own, Mila. Your father and I will wash our hands of you." Two days later, Ava and I were on a bus to Montana, where Grams welcomed us with open arms. I had never felt happier than I did at that moment. That was four years ago, and I haven't spoken to my parents since.

My mother doesn't even care enough to check in on her mother. Grams has been battling Alzheimer's for a couple of years now, and six months ago, I had to come to the difficult decision of placing her in a nursing home. Realizing I could no longer care for her by myself was one of the hardest days of my life. When Grams got the diagnosis, she made me promise not to burden myself with taking care of her. I told her I would never make that promise. When the time came to pick a nursing home for her, I chose the best facility we had in our area. Insurance pays for some, but I'm still left with a hefty sum each month, which is why I'm always snagging all the overtime I can. Grams deserves the best, no matter the cost.

With my thoughts of grabbing a coffee before my shift placed on the back burner, I head in the direction of Kate's office. Knocking, I wait for her permission to enter. "Come in!" she calls out. Opening the door, I see my boss typing away on her computer. "You wanted to see me?" I ask.

Taking her eyes off the screen, Kate slips her glasses off, placing them on the desk in front of her. "I did. Please come in, Mila, and have a seat."

Walking in, I shut the door behind me. "Is everything okay?" I ask, sitting down in the chair in front of her desk.

She sighs. "I'm afraid not. I hate to do this, but the hospital is making cutbacks, and unfortunately, nursing is the first to suffer. I'm being forced to let two nurses go. You were one of the last hired, so, in turn, one of the first I have to part with. I'm sorry, Mila. I hope you know that."

*Shit!*

What am I going to do? I was not expecting this when I came in this morning. Rubbing my sweaty palms on my leg, I nod. "I understand, Kate. I know it's not your fault. Will you at least call me if I'm able to come back? I like working here."

"I think I have something you might be interested in," she says, fumbling through the charts on her desk. Finding the one she was looking for, Kate hands it to me. Reaching across her desk, I take the offered file with a confused look.

"When I was handed this case this morning, I immediately thought of you. I know you took an In-Home Care course after your grandmother's diagnosis, so you are perfectly qualified for this job. The patient needs home care. He was involved in an accident about a month ago where he had been hit by a car."

My head snaps up with her description 'hit by a car.' *Is it him?* Looking down at the folder in my lap, I flip it open. Patient name —Reid Carter. My mouth goes dry at the sight of his name. I've only been around Reid a handful of times. All The Kings men make me a little nervous. They are not only ruthless but sweet, caring, and let's not forget utterly gorgeous. Especially the one in question. Reid stands at least six-foot-two, broad chest and shoulders. One of his arms is covered in colorful tattoos, and a few peek out from the collar of his shirts running up his neck. He also has hair the color of honey, and green eyes that cause my heart to flutter whenever he looks my way. The times I've ever been around him, he was mostly quiet. Always offering a quick greeting, but no real conversation. I don't take offense to it, though. I get the feeling he's more of an observer. He likes to study people.

As I scan Reid's chart, I listen to Kate discuss his injuries. Spinal swelling and a broken arm. "The patient has lost partial mobility in his left leg due to swelling pressing on the spinal nerves. He'll be doing physical therapy two to three days a week to start. You will need to take him to his sessions. He's not able to drive himself yet."

"What about his right leg? You said he lost mobility in his left leg. Does he have full function on the right?" I ask Kate.

Shaking her head, Kate replies, "The patient had an amputation of the right leg just below the knee from a previous accident. His doctor says Mr. Carter has been experiencing some tingling on that side, but can't move it. Being that he wears a prosthesis, his therapy will be a bit more challenging."

I'm shocked. I had no idea Reid wore a prosthetic. Bella and Alba never mentioned it. Then again, why would they? They would have no reason to. Kate, calling my name, draws my attention back to her. "There is something else you should know if you decide to take on this job."

I give her my full attention. "What?"

"Mila, the job is full-time, meaning it's live-in. Mr. Carter will require 24-hour care." I'm just about to protest when Kate jumps in. "I know you have your daughter, but at least go meet with Mr. Carter. Maybe you both can come up with an arrangement that will suit you both."

"Kate, it's just Ava and me. I don't have anyone I can depend on to help with my daughter. She's at preschool during the day, but I don't think anyone would take on a live-in nurse that comes with a child. I wouldn't ask them to."

"Would you be willing to meet with Mr. Carter, see if you two will be a good fit? If nothing else, I'll see about having another nurse stay during the night. But it might be a few weeks before I find someone. Are you okay with that?"

With a shaky breath, I accept. "Yes, I'll give it a try." At this point, I don't have a choice; I need the job.

"Great. Mr. Carter's address is in his file. Be there first thing in the morning."

Nodding my head in agreement, I stand up from my seat and head toward the door. Just as I'm about to reach for the knob, I turn back to Kate, "Has Reid—I mean Mr. Carter been told who his nurse will be?" I ask.

"No. Since I was just given the case this morning, I haven't had a chance to call and talk to him. But he is expecting you tomorrow morning."

"Okay. Thanks, Kate. I'll get in touch with you tomorrow after I meet with him." She smiles, and I leave her office.

Once the door shuts, I take three steps before I stop, lean my back against the wall and hug Reid's file to my chest as I take a deep breath. "This is not a big deal, Mila. You can do this. He's just another patient," I say to myself. A freaking hot as hell patient who happens to be a member of The Kings. I have a feeling I'm going to be in way over my head.

After stopping back by the nurse's station to pick up my purse and give Brittany the rundown of what just happened, I decided to spend the day with Grams.

When I walk into her room, Joni, her day nurse, gives me a warm smile.

"Well, what a nice surprise! We don't usually see you here so early. How you doin', sweetheart?" she asks, hugging me. I adore Joni. She's in her late 50's and has a warm vibe. Every time I see her, she greets me with a smile and a hug.

"I'm off work today, so I thought I'd come to sit with Grams for a little while. How is she doing today?"

She pats my arm. "She's okay. Been sleeping most of the morning. We had a bit of a rough night, so she's probably going to be out for a while." I don't have to ask. I know what Joni means by rough night. Grams would wake up in the middle of the night, calling and frantically looking for Grandpa. Having to tell her each time that Gramps was gone was heartbreaking. We lost Grandpa ten years ago to a heart attack. Now, every time Grandma has an episode, it's like losing him all over again.

Sighing, I look over at my grandmother's fragile frame sleeping soundly in her bed. I hate that the woman who has been like a mother to me, the woman who has molded me into the mother I am, has to suffer from such a horrible disease. And there is not a damn thing I can do about it.

"I'm just going to sit with her if that's okay," I say to Joni.

"Of course, sweetheart. I'll be back in a bit to check on her," she tells me as she slips out of the room.

Making my way over to the chair beside Grams' bed, I scoot it closer before sitting down. Reaching out, I place my hand on hers and watch the rise and fall of her chest. "I miss you so much, Grandma," I say, laying my head down next to her.

THE NEXT MORNING I'm running around the house trying to get ready and wrangle Ava out the door. I overslept. Which is something I never do. I don't want to look unprofessional on my first day of a new job. I don't want Reid to have a bad impression of me. I take my career very seriously.

"Ava!" I holler down the hallway, "It's time to go, sweet girl." Hearing my little girl giggle as she runs down the hall with her blonde curls bouncing makes me smile.

"I'm ready, Momma," she announces, looking up at me with her big blue eyes. My baby looks nothing like me. I have a pale complexion, long, straight black hair, and light brownish-yellow almond-shaped eyes. People tell me all the time my eyes remind them of a cat's eyes. Ava has sun-kissed skin, beautiful blonde curly hair, and big blue eyes. *Just like her father.*

My daughter has a bubbly personality and no filter. She usually says exactly what's on her mind, whereas I tend to keep my thoughts to myself. I suppose it's something I learned as a child. I was taught at a young age; my parents had no tolerance for my opinions. What I thought or wanted didn't matter. That is why I embrace Ava's boldness. I want her to speak her mind, to say what she is thinking and what she's feeling.

I remember the first summer I spent with Grams. I hardly spoke. She would try to engage me in conversation, and I would give my standard one-word answers. At six years old, my grandmother sat me down and explained to me that when I was with her, I was allowed to speak freely, that she wanted to know everything. What my favorite TV show was, what I like to do for fun, how I like school. Grams wanted to know it all.

When I got older, she confided in me, telling me how much it pained her that my mom had changed so much after meeting my father. It hadn't taken long before my mother began acting as if she was too good to be associated with her own family and where she grew up. Grams said it was because of me she tried to keep the peace with my mother. She knew if she didn't put up with my mother and father, she would never see me. Although I think it was the other way around. I believe my parents kept a small relationship with Grams, so they had somewhere to dump me when they didn't want me around. I would never let on how much I loved coming to Montana. I was always worried they would see how happy I was and snatch it away from me.

A tug on my shirttail brings me out of my thoughts.

"Momma, your face looks funny."

Looking down at Ava, I stick my tongue out at her. "*Your* face looks funny." Ruffling the hair on top of her head, I tip my head in the direction of the door. "Come on silly girl, let's go before we're late."

Thirty minutes later, after dropping Ava off at preschool, I find myself at the address in Reid's file. Confused, I look out my window at the building in front of me and then back down at the address in the file. Yep, this is the right place. What's confusing is that it's not a house or an apartment. Currently, I'm parked in front of an old firehouse with two large roll-up doors, typical for a fire station, and on the side of the building is a set of stairs leading to a metal door. I guess I'll take my chances with the side entrance.

Stepping out of my car, I sling my purse over my shoulder before shutting my door. I don't bother locking it. My car is a rusted piece of crap and is on its last leg. Even though this part of town looks a little sketchy, I don't worry about anyone wanting to steal it. Besides, if everyone knows who lives here, then I'm sure they would not have the audacity to mess around the home of a local MC member.

When I reach the top of the stairs, I look up to my right and notice a camera pointed directly at me. I've heard Bella mention Reid is a techie, so I'm pretty sure I'm in the right place. He probably has cameras all over the place. Pressing the buzzer next to the door, I wait. It takes five more times of ringing the doorbell before the door is pulled open, and I'm face to face with a very gorgeous, and very pissed off looking Reid.

"What the hell do you want?" he sneers.

# 3

## REID

I wake up to someone persistently ringing my doorbell the next morning. Grabbing my phone from the nightstand, I read the time, 9:15 am. It's been four weeks since I've gotten to sleep past 6 o'clock because, for once, no one came in flipping on lights, bothering me to take medication, and so on, and now some asshole is ringing my doorbell. I pull up the app on my phone, synced to the camera located at the entrance of the building only to see Bella's friend Mila standing there.

*What the hell is she doing here?*

I take a few seconds to look at her. Mila is five-foot-six with raven black hair that hangs past her shoulders. She is slim with curves in all the right places and a heart-shaped face paired with the most amazing eyes I'd ever seen, and I'm obsessed with her mouth and how her bottom lip is slightly fuller than the top.

The first time I met her was at a BBQ out at the clubhouse. She and her little girl that is. No one has ever stolen my breath or left me at a loss for words like she does. I'll never forget the first time she looked at me with her cat-like eyes. Never had I seen eyes like hers before. She stole my fuckin' breath away. Regardless, there is no reason for her to be at my doorstep, and I want her gone. I can't have her staring at me. Judging me. Not her.

She reaches out, ringing the doorbell again. I throw the blankets to the foot of the bed, pull myself up, and shift my legs over the edge and slide over into my chair. Dressed in only my sweatpants from the day before, I head out of my room, into the hallway, and make my way into the kitchen. In an agitated state, I fling open my door. "What the hell do you want?" I bark at her, my voice gruff from sleepiness.

Her hypnotizing eyes connect with mine and hold my stare for a beat before she responds, "You mind letting me in first before I explain why I'm here?" she says, sounding pissed.

She's out here ringing my damn doorbell, waking me up, and she's pissed off? "What do you want? I'm not in the mood for visitors," I tell her.

"InCare sent me."

What? Hell no. This isn't going to work. I won't have Mila doing those things for me. "No," I clip.

"No?" she answers a bit taken aback by my attitude, but she quickly recovers. "Look, I admit, I had some reservations at first when I was given your file yesterday, but I need this job, Reid." When Mila crosses her arms over her chest, the move pushes her ample chest up further, causing my attention to shift briefly. "I'm also not going to stand here and beg either," she retorts, giving me a little attitude in return.

I bring my eyes back up to her face only to see her glaring back at me. "I understand the requirements are full-time for at least four to eight weeks, depending on recovery time. Am I correct?"

"You read the chart, Kitten, so I would assume you already know that." I continue to stare at her and notice her eyes flare in irritation at my calling her Kitten. "I'm not a damn pet. I have a name," she hisses. "So, I would appreciate you using it."

"Nah, I think I like Kitten better," I interject with a grin and watch as her face reddens, and she balls her fists up at her side. When I open my mouth to retort, I'm effectively cut off by the raise of her hand. Not many people would get away with that shit, but Mila doing it shows me she's got a nice set of lady balls, and I can respect that.

"My daughter would have to come too," she grinds out through clenched teeth, ignoring my last statement.

I'm not prepared to deal with the noise and hassle involved with a kid running around my home. *Shit.* No matter what my mixed-up feelings are about my current situation or the fact that I'm crazy attracted to the woman standing in front of me, I'm not going to be the reason she can't take care of her little girl. Giving in, for now, I make my way to the kitchen table, and she follows. Pulling a chair out, she takes a seat.

"You realize what you're in for? I'm not a small man, Mila." I gesture to myself with my hands. "You may have to help me get in and out of things like this chair, a vehicle—" I pause and try to hide a grin. "—the shower. And sometimes I need help getting my clothes on. It's not something I want to be done for me, but with one good arm..." I shrug my shoulders, keeping eye contact with her.

She scans my body. And it doesn't go unnoticed, she didn't linger on my leg. Most women do. They keep staring as if it's an alien life form or something, but she didn't.

Clearing her throat, she sits up straighter. "I'm more than capable of doing all those things, Mr. Carter. It's my job, and I'm pretty good at it."

*Oh. It's Mr. Carter now.* "I thought you were an OB nurse?" I question her.

"I'm certified in in-home care as well. I wouldn't have been sent here if I wasn't qualified."

"Alright, then I'll give it one week for you to show me you can handle it," I respond.

Relaxing, Mila leans back in her chair. "I apologize for waking you this morning. I can make some coffee if you like?" She scans the room then stands, making her way to the counter where the coffee pot sits.

I watch the way she moves as she makes her way to the counter. "Sounds like a good start."

*What have I got myself into?*

"I can find my way around the kitchen. You can get dressed if you want. Put on a shirt," she says, opening and closing cabinets until she finds what she needs.

Maybe I make her just as uncomfortable as she makes me.

"That's okay, Kitten. I'm good."

Her back stiffens when the word Kitten leaves my mouth once again but chooses to ignore it this time. She shrugs her shoulders, "Suit yourself. Are you hungry? I could cook something. It's all part of my job description." Walking over to the fridge, she opens it, only to find some expired coffee creamer and a jar of mayonnaise. "Or maybe not," she mumbles, closing the door.

"I need to get some groceries. Quinn was here and found what food I did have was all spoiled before leaving yesterday." I say, rubbing the back of my neck with my hand and recalling his face when he took a bite of the bad lunch meat he had slapped on to some bread while making a sandwich yesterday. Mila lets out a soft laugh that surprisingly relaxes me enough to smile as well.

"Yeah, I've noticed the few times I've been around Quinn he's always eating."

"Come on. I'll show you around while we wait for the coffee," I offer. "As you can see, this is the kitchen and living room area."

We make our way toward the hallway. I stop at the spare room and open the door, moving my chair enough for her to squeeze by and look inside. The room is empty. I've had no reason to have furniture put in there. Until now. As she brushes by me, I inhale, breathing in her scent.

"Did you just sniff me?" Mila turns to face me.

"It's called breathing. You're a nurse. You should know the basic functions of the human body," I smart off, and move further down the hall, showing her the bathroom. "It's all yours. I have my own in my bedroom." Continuing the tour, I give her a short-clipped conversation. Stopping, I show her the master bedroom. She walks around and takes in the equipment I had installed yesterday before stepping into the bathroom.

"I'm happy to see you are trying to do some things on your own, but that shower is an accident waiting to happen," she says walking back out from looking at the shower stall. "You really should get a non-slip shower stool to sit on and not that tiled bench seat. Oh, and one of those non-slip tub mats too," she states.

"It has those rails to hold on to, and I've always used the built-in bench," I tell her.

"If I'm going to be helping lift your wet body in and out of the shower, it needs to be safer for not only you, Reid, but me as well," she says with a slight blush on her face.

"I should show you downstairs too. That is where my office is and where I spend most of my time. Follow me." I take her to the elevator and motion for her to get in.

"That thing doesn't look safe. I'll take the stairs." She looks on as I position my chair.

"It's safe, get on." Slowly she steps beside me, and I pull the rod iron gate closed, push the button, and the elevator makes a slow, short descent to the bottom. "My office is just over there," I point.

Without going across the room, I inform her, "It's the only place off limits around here. If I'm down here, don't bother me."

Mila looks around then turns and studies me for a moment. I fully expect her to pry, but she doesn't, which surprises me.

"Let's go have some coffee," she says and turns, taking the stairs up instead, leaving me alone to think for a few moments. I've got no reasons to not trust her yet. If anything, I'm not sure I can trust myself with her.

When I get back to the kitchen, Quinn shows up. "Let me in, asshole," he says through the intercom.

Opening the door, I let him in and see he is holding a couple of boxes of doughnuts, and standing behind him is Charley. "Grabbed some breakfast on my way here, and this old man followed me trying to steal my food," he jokes.

"Hey, son. Good to see they let your ass out of the hospital. You look like shit, though. You need to roll your ass into the shower and trim up that shit on your face," Charley pokes fun as he leans down for a hug.

"Whose piece of shit car is parked in the driveway out there?" Quinn asks, gesturing with his thumb over his shoulder.

"That would be mine," Mila chimes in walking out of the hallway.

Great, now Quinn has a shit-eating grin on his face. I give him a look telling him to shut the fuck up before he tries to open his mouth, and I pray he listens for once.

Charley looks confused because he has no idea who Mila is and why I would have a woman in my home.

"Mila is going to be my in-home nurse," I reluctantly inform him.

"No, shit? You're a lucky son of a bitch." Quinn grins at me.

"Quinn," I warn him. He's good at keeping his trap shut when it counts, but something like this is pure gold for his gossip hole. Now that he knows, so will everyone else. I don't know which is worse right now. The woman I've been crazy attracted to ever since the first day I saw her moving in as my nurse, or dipshit here running his mouth and knowing I'm going to catch all kinds of hell from the rest of my brothers before the day is through.

"Where are your manners, Reid. You gonna introduce me or what?" Charley chastises.

"Charley, this Mila. Mila, this is Charley," I quickly introduce them. Charley is like my second dad. He was my old man's best friend. I'm talking since birth they were the best of friends, that's how long they knew each other. Wiping her hands on a napkin, Mila throws a partially eaten cinnamon twist into the garbage can and extends her hand to greet him. "Nice to meet you, Charley."

"You too," he returns

Turning to look at me, Mila says, "How about I go do some grocery shopping and let you fellas do your thing?"

"Get my bank card, it's in my wallet on my dresser in the bedroom," I tell her.

She disappears down the hall then reappears, holding my wallet. "Here, I'm not going into your wallet," she says, handing it to me. I open it and pull out my card, handing it to her. "Anything specific I should pick up? Likes or dislikes?" she inquires.

Right now, with Quinn and Charley looking on, I want her gone. "No, and bring the receipt back," I grump, feeling uncomfortable.

Seeming unfazed, she walks to the table, grabs her purse, and walks out the door. Both Quinn and Charley stare at me. I roll to the counter and start fixing a cup of coffee with the mug Mila had taken down from the cabinet.

"What's wrong with you this morning?" Charley gruffs.

"What?" I clip.

"The fuckin' attitude you're sporting? Have you been treating that girl like that all morning?" he asks.

"Damn it, Charley. I don't need any of this shit right now."

Quinn picks up one of the doughnut boxes and tucks it under his arm, "I'm gonna get. Go easy on her, Reid. She's only here to do her job," he says. "See ya later, brother."

"See there, your cranky ass is running everyone off," Charley points out.

28

I take my coffee back to the table, set it down, and run my hand down my face. He's right. My moods are all over the place.

"You need to get your head out of your ass and stop feeling sorry for yourself. That's where all this shit is coming from. Self-pity. Your dad didn't raise you to treat a woman with such little respect. Even though it's her job to care for you, she doesn't deserve that kind of behavior. I came here thinking I could have a nice visit with my godson, but now I have a bad taste in my mouth, and that's because of you." He snatches the other box of doughnuts off the table. "And I'm taking these with me." He walks toward the door, "I'm always here for you, son, so when you decide to pull that stick out of your ass, you give me a call."

Left sitting alone in my kitchen, I think over the verbal beating I just received. He's right; Dad would be mad as hell right now. Taking myself to my bathroom, I stare at my reflection in the mirror. I do look like shit. I haven't shaved since being in the hospital, and I usually keep all my facial hair trimmed short. I grab my beard trimmer and get to work. Once I'm done, I forgo a shower because the more I look at the bench, the more I think about Mila being right about not trusting that slick tile. Some deodorant and cologne will have to do for now. I wheel myself to my dresser and pull a shirt from the drawer and slip it over my cast and my head.

Knowing I need to show my gratitude and apologize, I decide to furnish the spare room for Mila and her daughter. Grabbing my laptop, I go into the living room. Sitting the computer on the coffee table, I position my chair as close as I can get it to the couch and slide myself over onto it. Opening my laptop, I get to work. I'm not entirely sure what her or her daughter will like, so I pick things out and hope for the best. Once I'm through with my purchase, the furniture store emails a confirmation that they should have everything delivered late this evening.

Realizing I forgot to give it to her before she left, I grab my phone from the coffee table and text Mila the security code, so she can come and go as she pleases, then realize I don't have her number. No problem. I open a new window on my computer screen, go into a few systems, and snag her cell number.

*Me: This is Reid. Security Code to get back in 52469. Remember, then delete the text. I'll be downstairs for the rest of the day.*

I WAIT FOR HER RESPONSE, which I receive about three minutes later.

*Mila: I'm not going to ask how you got my number. I'm done at the store. I'll cook you something to eat when I get back.*

Unsure what to say, I don't reply. I take myself and my coffee downstairs to my office, hoping I can get my mind off Mila for a while.

Engrossed in my work, the time seems to pass quickly, and before I know it, I'm smelling something delicious, and my stomach rumbles. Closing everything down, I load up on the elevator and head back upstairs. I find Mila ladling what smells like chili into a couple of containers by the stove. Lifting her head, she watches as I wheel over to the kitchen island.

"I didn't know if you like chili or not, but I made a small batch. I left some for you to eat now if you like, and the rest I'll put in the refrigerator."

Finding my words, I thank her. "I appreciate it."

I watch her place leftovers in the refrigerator and then load the dishwasher. "You staying? I mean—you want to eat something too?" I fumble over my words. *Shit, what am I ten years old?*

"No, I need to go pick up Ava and start getting things ready for us to come and stay here. That is if you still want me to. I called my supervisor earlier, and she is more than happy to send another nurse for the night who can help you out. If you need it," she tells me.

I think I want to be alone for the rest of the night. Besides, it gives me time to get her room set up. "You go on. And I'm still willing to give this a try. I'll call InCare and let them know I won't need anyone tonight. I'll give Quinn a call. He'll sack out on the couch and be here if I need anything," I let her know as she's gathering her purse and keys.

"Then, I'll see you tomorrow?"

"Yeah." I nod my head.

She gives me a slight smile. "Okay. I'll see you later, Reid."

Again, I'm left alone, which is what I thought I've wanted for weeks.

The truth is, I don't want her to go.

# 4

## MILA

Today is the day. The day I move in with Reid. No big deal, right? It's only for a few weeks. I know Reid was reluctant with me staying, considering I have Ava, and if he said no, I would have understood. I'm aware not too many people would have been willing to accommodate a live-in nurse with a small child. I can't believe Kate would even suggest me for the job. What the hell was she thinking? After leaving Reid's place yesterday, I almost called my boss. I wanted to tell her she should find someone else, but the bigger picture is I need the money. I have bills and responsibilities. It's because of Ava and Grams that I'm going to suck it up and do the job. Kate wouldn't have chosen me if she didn't think I could handle it. I need to learn not to take Reid's attitude personally. I mean, who can blame the guy? My job is to help him get better, and that is precisely what I am going to do. If Reid Carter thinks I can't handle his brash words and sour attitude, then he's sorely mistaken.

Growing up the way I did has given me a thick skin. I can take whatever he throws at me. Besides, I have a feeling what I saw yesterday is not who Reid is. I don't know all the struggles he has faced in his life, but I know lost when I see it. I'm only there to help him recover, that's it. I have enough problems of my own than to be worried about that man. That gorgeous sexy—"Ugh, stop it, Mila," I chastise myself. "He's not that sexy," I lie to myself while looking down at the suitcases I have open on top of my bed. And never mind the fact that my stomach flutters every time he calls me Kitten.

This morning I explained to Ava the best way I knew how what was happening. I told her we are going to stay with a friend for a little while, so Mommy can help him get better. She looked at me for a moment then asked if she could bring her princess pillow and princess blanket. When I told her of course, she happily went back to eating her cereal.

An hour later, she was dropped off at preschool, and I came back home to finish packing. After staring at these suitcases for the past fifteen minutes, I decide what I need is a pep talk. And I know just who to talk to. Pulling my phone from my back pocket, I fire off a text.

*Me: Want to grab a coffee?*

My phone pings seconds later.

*Bella: YES!!! I thought you'd never ask!*

When I read her reply, I shake my head and chuckle. I'm betting Bella knows exactly why I want to meet. She has probably already heard the news of me being Reid's home care nurse from Quinn since he was at Reid's place yesterday. I bet she's been dying to talk to me and was waiting for me to say something first.

I couldn't ask for a better friend than Bella. A couple of years ago, before she met Logan, she started working at the grocery store in town. I had started working there about a month before her, and we became instant friends. She has Logan and the club now, and I don't feel right taking up too much of her time. When I do need a shoulder to lean on or someone to talk to, Bella always drops everything to be there for me.

Gathering my keys and my purse, I walk out of the house I've shared with my grandmother for the past few years and make my way to my car. I drive to the coffee shop, which is only a few miles away. When I pull up, I can see Bella through the front window of the store. She watches me get out of my car with the biggest smile on her face. *Yep, she knows.*

Pushing the shop door open, I see she already has my coffee waiting for me. I barely take my seat at the table across from her when she speaks up. "Anything new?"

Rolling my eyes, I take a sip of my coffee, "Like you don't already know."

"Of course, I know. Quinn told me. Don't let their cuts fool you, those men gossip like a bunch of fifteen-year-old girls," she softly laughs. A mental picture of a bunch of bikers sitting around gossiping like a bunch of housewives makes me giggle right along with her.

"Alright," Bella says, looking serious. "Jokes aside, are you okay with being Reid's caretaker? Quinn said he was a bit difficult. I promise you, Mila, that's not how Reid normally acts. He's having a hard time." She raises her hand, stopping me before I protest. "I know it's no excuse for his behavior, but I want you to know that. And how did all this happen? Are you not working at the hospital anymore?"

I wave my hand at her, "I don't take his attitude personally. I deal with patients like him all the time. I know it's not me he's angry with, it's his situation. I promise you; I can handle Reid." After Bella studies the sincerity of my response, I continue to tell her about losing my job and my boss giving me Reid's case.

"You know I'm a firm believer that all things happen for a reason," Bella utters from behind her mug. She has a wicked gleam in her eye too.

"Bella Kane, don't you go getting any ideas in that head of yours. It's just a job. Nothing more." I can tell by her secretive smile she won't be letting this go. The last thing I want is Bella playing matchmaker. If the constant sneer Reid was sending my way yesterday was any indication, he's not the least bit interested either.

Thirty minutes later, Bella and I part with plans to meet up again in a couple of days. I already feel so much better. Sometimes all you need is a good friend to lean on and someone to tell you everything will be okay.

Later that day, I have mine and Ava's things packed and in my car when I go to pick her up from preschool. We are now on our way to Reid's. The drive to his place is short as I listen to Ava jabber in the rear seat about her day.

"Is dis it, Momma?" Ava asks, pointing out the window.

"Yeah, baby girl, this is it." Getting out of the car, I open the back door and unstrap Ava from her car seat.

"How ya doin', darlin'?" A deep voice says from behind me, making me jump, and I bang my head on the roof of my car.

"Damn it!" I shout.

"Oh, shit, sweetheart. Didn't mean to scare ya."

When I turn around, I see Quinn standing behind me, holding his hands up and wincing. "I saw you pull up. Thought I'd come down and help you carry your stuff up."

"It's okay, Quinn," I tell him while rubbing the knot on the top of my head. "And some help would be great, thanks." Leaning back down in the car, I lift Ava out of her seat and sat her down on the ground.

"Momma, you say a bad word."

"I know, baby, I'm sorry. Now come on, let's get our stuff inside, okay?" Doing as I ask, she walks around to the trunk of my car. When my daughter sees Quinn standing there, she stops in her tracks and looks up at him. "Hi," she greets, not acting shy at all.

"How ya doin' kid?"

She studies him for several seconds before opening her mouth as she says what I knew was coming. "You say a bad word too." Quinn looks to me for guidance. I offer him a shrug. He turns back to Ava, and I watch as he opens and closes his mouth a few times at a loss for words. He takes his wallet out of his back pocket and pulls out a dollar. "Sorry, kid, here ya go." And hands her the money. With a sly smile, my little girl takes the offered dollar and stuffs it in her pocket.

"I forgive you." When I look back at Quinn, he has a huge smile plastered on his face as if he's won. When he looks back at me, I shake my head at him. "Big, big mistake."

His smile quickly turns into a frown. "What?"

"Oh, you'll see," I tell him, patting his arm as I walk by. The three of us walk side by side through the entrance on the ground floor. Stepping onto the lift, Quinn presses the button that takes us up to the top.

"Dis is so cool," Ava gushes. "We get to lib here, Momma?"

"We sure do!" I say trying to sound excited for my little girl, only I'm not the least bit excited, I'm nervous as hell. Stepping off the lift, I peer around the room looking for Reid.

"He's in his room," Quinn informs me. "He'll probably be out in a bit. Until then, let's get you settled in your room." He motions down the hall.

"Come on, baby, this way," I tell Ava as we both follow Quinn. I wasn't expecting our room to be furnished. The first thing I notice is a queen-size bed, and on the opposite side of the room is a toddler bed. Everything here looks new. I can't believe Reid did this for us. I would have been fine on a pull-out or an air bed. Quinn seems to be reading my expression because he speaks up.

"He wanted you both to be comfortable. Contrary to his current attitude, Reid is one of the best guys I know. Don't let him fool ya."

Not having any response to that, I simply nod. Dipping his head, Quinn turns to leave. "I'm going to get out of here and let you all settle in."

"Thanks, Quinn, I appreciate your help."

Stopping, he turns around, "Anytime, darlin'. And a piece of advice. Give him hell. Whatever he dishes out, you give it back ten-fold."

Later in the evening, Ava and I venture out into the kitchen. Reid still hasn't made an appearance. I know he's okay because I can hear his TV, and it sounded like he was talking to someone on the phone earlier. Either way, Ava needs her dinner. It's weird being in someone else's space and using their things. "Want to help momma cook dinner?"

"Yes!" Ava squeals, clapping her hands together. Looking through the fully stocked cabinets and freezer, I turn to my little helper. "How about spaghetti?" Watching her vigorously nodding her head, I believe she agrees. Spotting a step stool in the corner, I bring it over to the kitchen island for Ava. We go about mixing our ingredients for the sauce, and then I move on to start the water for the noodles. I love cooking with my daughter. Grams used to let me cook with her every day I was at her house. She taught me everything I know, including this homemade sauce. Grams never used the stuff from a can. I usually like to let my sauce simmer for most of the day, but this will do in a pinch.

Roughly an hour later, I'm pulling the garlic bread from the oven while Ava sets the table when I'm startled by movement in the hall.

I look over my shoulder and notice Reid watching us with a weird look on his face. When he sees I've caught him, the look he had before vanishes. I'm the first to break the silence. "Dinner is almost done if you're hungry." He makes his way over to the dining room table.

"I could eat."

I give him a small smile.

It's a start.

# 5

## REID

I would be lying if I said sitting here in the hallway and watching Mila shuffle around my kitchen cooking dinner didn't spark something profound inside of me. I would be lying if I said I didn't feel a pull toward her. Watching my brothers Logan and Gabriel with their women, and seeing how happy they are, makes me a little envious. Don't get me wrong; I'm beyond thrilled for them. They're both good men and deserve a good woman, but I'm envious because I know I may never have that. Especially with a woman like Mila. Beautiful, caring, and a great mother. A woman like her is out of my reach. Before the car accident where I lost my leg, I wouldn't have thought twice about going after a woman like her, but now...

About a year after I lost my leg, I started seeing a woman. I'll never forget the look of pity and disgust on her face when I told her about my prosthesis. We'd been dating for two months. I know she wanted to take the next step, so I finally worked up the nerve to tell her about my leg. Three emotions swept across her face. Shock, pity, and then disgust. I never saw her again. She's not a local living in Polson, she lives a few towns over, so at least we don't have to cross paths. *Fuckin' bitch.*

Since then, when I need to take the edge off, I'll go to Charley's. There's plenty of willing women looking for a good time with a biker. I don't pay for pussy—never have, never will. Is a quick fuck in a bar bathroom, or having my cock sucked by a club whore my idea of satisfying? Hell no. But I'll be damned if I let another woman look at me with pity ever again.

Hearing someone gasp pulls me from my thoughts. That's when I notice Mila has stopped what she was doing and is looking at me. We hold each other's stare for a beat before she speaks. "Dinner will be done soon if you're hungry," she says nervously. Rolling toward the dining room table, I inform her, "I could eat."

I'll admit the smell of whatever she's cooking drew me out of my room. I know I've been a dick, hiding out like I've been doing. But I would rather be alone than lash out at Mila. Hurting her feelings is the last thing I want to do. When Quinn was here earlier, he had no problem pointing out to me I was a reclusive asshole. He was right. No matter what I may be dealing with, I have no right taking it out on the people around me. It's just the shocking realization Mila was going to be my nurse threw me for a fuckin' loop. The nurse I had in the hospital didn't affect me. She was a no-nonsense motherly type. Mila, on the other hand, does shit to me. Every time those hypnotizing eyes look at me, my insides clench. That alone pisses me off. I can't stand the thought of any woman having the power to make me feel anything.

"Are you going to eat wif me and Momma, Mr. Carter?" I hear a tiny voice ask. Looking to my right, I see Ava standing there holding a plate and looking up at me with the biggest blue eyes.

"Yeah, sweetheart. I'm going to eat supper with ya. Is that okay?" I can't help but chuckle when she bobs her head, and her blonde curls bounce all over her face. A few minutes later, the three of us have settled, and I am eating some of the best spaghetti I have ever tasted.

"Did you like the sgeti, Mr. Carter? I helped Momma make it."

Turning my gaze away from Mila, who has begun clearing the dishes from the table, I look at a spaghetti-covered Ava. "Best I ever had, sweetheart. And if it's okay with your momma, you can call me Reid." When Ava looks over at her mom, Mila gives her a nod. Then Ava turns back to me giving me a toothy smile. I am so out of my element when it comes to kids. But I at least try.

"I'm going to turn in," I announce, backing up from the table.

Placing the dishes in the sink, Mila strides toward me. "I'll help you."

"I got it," I bite out a bit too roughly, causing Mila to jump. Clearing my throat, I glance back at her and sigh. "I'm sorry, Kitten. What I meant was, I'm good. I'll see you two in the mornin'." When I see Mila step away from me with a hurt look on her face, I instantly feel like a dick.

Ignoring the pinch in my gut, I continue to my room. I was telling her the truth when I said I could get to bed on my own. I look like a fumbling idiot, but I want to be able to do some shit for myself. The two things I refuse help with are using the bathroom and getting myself to bed. A week before leaving the hospital, I gained some feeling in my right leg. With my prosthetic on, I can balance my weight on that one side for a few moments at a time. I am so fucking thankful for that too.

Letting out a deep sigh, I close my eyes and think about the events that led me here. I don't for one-second regret doing whatever needed to be done to help Alba. I know she blames herself for what that sick motherfucker did to me, but I would go through the events all over again if it meant saving the life of just one person I care about. My only regret—I failed her. The psycho was still able to get to her and Leyna. I failed them both, just like I failed my brother Noah.

I'm determined to get better. I need to prove to my club that they can count on me. When I lost my leg, I thought for sure my days as a King were over. The thought of not being a part of the club, of not being able to ever ride again, made me want to put a bullet in my head. I came damn close one time. I let self-pity control my decisions. Until Quinn saved me. It's like my brother knew something wasn't right with me.

It was about six months after the accident that killed my brother. I had the day all planned out. I just wanted it all to be over. I felt like I could not take the pain of losing Noah anymore. I was sitting in my apartment on the evening I was planning on eating a bullet when Quinn unexpectedly stopped by. He walked through my door, and his eyes zeroed in on my piece, which was lying on the kitchen counter, along with a single bullet sitting beside it. He took one hard look at me and told me, "That shit's not happenin', brother." He stayed with me the whole night, and the next day he showed back up with several bags. Quinn took it upon himself to move in and become my babysitter. Fuck, I was pissed. Who the hell was he to take over my life and tell me what I could and couldn't do?

Two months later, I had never been more grateful. Quinn saved my life. We haven't spoken of it since. My other brothers have never mentioned it either. I'm not sure if Quinn ever told them what happened. I never did. All I know is he brought me back to a good place, and I'll be forever indebted to him. The amazing thing about Quinn is, he knows people. He has some sort of intuition. And he always acts on it.

The memory of when Logan and I met Quinn still makes me shake my head. Quinn and his family moved to Polson when we were in high school. Logan and I were ditching class and had passed by the boy's bathroom when we heard a commotion. When we walked in, we saw a skinny blond-haired runt getting the shit beat out of him. One thing I can't stand is a fucking bully. Anyway, I pulled the bigger kid off the smaller kid, and then Logan and I gave him a taste of his own medicine. When we were finished with the asshole, he scurried out of the bathroom with a busted lip and a bruised eye. We both turned our attention to the kid who was standing against the wall holding his ribs.

"What's your name?" I had asked him. The skinny kid wiped the blood from his lip, "Quinn," he replied.

"Well, Quinn, that fucker won't be botherin' you anymore."

Logan and I turned to leave when Quinn hollered out, "Hey, wait up!"

From that day on, Quinn became our shadow. Here we had this skinny little runt following us around. No matter what, we couldn't shake him. He's not a skinny little runt anymore. But he's still a shithead, and I wouldn't want him any other way.

---

I'M ROLLING down the hall the next morning when I hear laughter. A smile tugs at my lips when I hear Mila trying to hush Ava.

"She's alright, Mila. I've been up for hours," I say. The sound of my voice startles her. Throwing her hand over her chest and letting out a shriek, Mila spins around to face me.

"Jesus Christ, Reid. Anyone ever tell you-you're like a ghost?"

"Sorry, Kitten," I apologize in a slightly amused tone. Today Mila is in a pair of navy blue scrub bottoms that on most people would be unflattering, but not Mila. She has paired it with a simple long sleeved black thermal top that fits snug across her breasts, and her midnight hair is pulled up into a high ponytail. When my eyes land on her face, I see a pink tint to her cheeks. She has obviously caught me checking her out. *What the hell am I doing?*

Wiping the smile off my face, I turn away from her and make my way into the kitchen for some coffee. Mila is here to be my nurse, and here I am, acting like a fucking pervert. After a few awkward moments, Mila is the first to speak.

"Your first PT appointment is at 8:30 am. We can drop Ava off at preschool on our way, if that's okay?"

Rolling past her, I nod my head, "I'll be downstairs."

---

I FEEL like my body is on fire. We just got back home from my first PT appointment, and all I want is to take a shower and go to bed. As soon as we got home, the first thing Mila did was fix me some lunch. She went to the refrigerator, pulled out some leftovers from the night before, along with coconut water. Walking over, she sets a plate in front of me.

"Thanks," I mutter.

Picking her purse and keys up off the counter, Mila makes her way toward the door. "I need to pick Ava up from preschool. It'll only be about fifteen minutes. Will you be okay till I get back?"

"I'll be fine. I'm going to eat and then probably turn in early."

Mila is quiet for a moment while she studies my face. "I should be back before you finish your lunch. Then I will help you get settled. Your PT was hard on you today Reid—"

Before she can finish her sentence, I cut her off. "I said I'd be fine," I defend, my tone sharp. Thinning her lips, Mila nods before shutting the door behind her. "God fucking damn it!" I roar and shove my plate across the table. My lunch forgotten, I wheel myself down the hall to my bedroom and into my bathroom, stopping in front of my walk-in shower. Leaning over, I turn the hot water on and wait as it heats up. Minutes later, I'm still sitting in my chair as the steam from the hot water fills the room. I'm so fucking tired and so fucking weak. I'm a grown-ass man that can't even shower himself. How fucking pathetic.

I don't know how long I have been sitting here when I hear a light knock on the bathroom door. "Reid?" Mila's soft voice calls through the door. I don't have it in me to answer. And I don't have it in me to look up when I hear the click of the knob turning and the door opening.

# 6

## MILA

The ride back to Reid's place earlier today after his therapy session was filled with silence. Both of us were probably lost in our thoughts, or at least I know I was. All in all, his first session went well. Hopefully, his attitude gets better with time, especially toward accepting my help. I know he has some issues, hell, we all do, but having a sour attitude toward it all will only affect his recovery process negatively. Life is hard in general, and sometimes we have to overcome more than one speed bump in life. Sometimes a whole damn wall is standing in our way. But you find a way to climb over it and carry on. I, for one, will never let something get in the way of my happiness—for myself or my daughter.

Ava left some of her toys on the floor this morning and I didn't get them picked up. By the sour look on Reid's face, he wasn't pleased with the small mess. I'm used to it and overlook her things scattered here and there. Sure, it used to bug me, and I would constantly be cleaning up after her, but with an almost-five-year-old, it's nearly impossible to keep a clean home. I need to remember Reid isn't used to it and pay better attention to her messes while I'm on this assignment.

Sighing, I reach over and crank up the radio. A few minutes to myself as I head to pick Ava up, leaving Reid alone at his place, is just what I need at the moment. I need to de-stress and a nice bubble bath after I put Ava down tonight is starting to sound like a perfect plan. All these thoughts and events of my day are running through my head as I pull into the parking lot outside Ava's preschool. Taking a deep breath, trying to release a little of the tension in my neck and shoulders, I shut the engine off and climb out of my car.

Walking inside, I'm met by another mother, Claire Walker, who has her three-year-old son in tow.

*Please walk by*, I silently plead.

"Hello, Mila. How are you today?" she says with an annoyingly high-pitched voice. She is one of those moms with her perfectly put together outfit, perfectly styled hair, and makeup. The kind you would never catch in a pair of sweatpants and a messy bun piled on top of their head and wearing a hint of makeup from the day before. "Hi, Claire," I slightly wave my hand at her and attempt to continue on my way.

"Liam mentioned they had to make cutbacks, and the hospital had to let you go. So sorry to hear that." She fake smiles.

I do my best to bite my tongue. First, I know her husband, Liam, Dr. Walker, didn't say anything to her. He's not the gossip type. She had to have heard it elsewhere. Second, Claire seems to think I want her husband, so she has a habit of knowing whatever she can about me, and it pisses me off. "I appreciate your concern," I return with a forced smile of my own.

"You still plan on attending the charity ball this year? Formal invites went out two weeks ago. The charity this year is Alzheimer's. I wanted to give again to last year's charity, but Liam insisted we give to different charities throughout the community every year." She lets out a bored sigh as she looks at her manicured nails.

My contribution won't be much. A hundred dollars at best, but the cause is very near and dear to my heart. Ever since I've been on this journey alongside Grams, I have tried to contribute in any way possible to help fight this terrible disease. So, I'm going for that very reason to give my Grams a voice. The nurses at the hospital, my friends, they know about my grandmother and the struggles we go through. They think I would be the perfect representative to give a speech at the charity function. Not wanting her to stick her nose into any more of my business, I stay clear of answering her question. "I'm sorry I can't stay and talk, Claire. I need to get Ava, so if you'll excuse me," I tell her as pleasantly as possible.

"Oh, well, of course," she replies dryly, obviously annoyed that I have just dismissed her. Stepping around Claire, I head toward the classroom where my daughter is waiting for me.

"Momma, Momma!" Ava comes skipping across the room from where she was sitting with a piece of paper flapping around in her hand. "Momma, look, I got to use magic today!" she cheerfully says as she shows me the artwork in her hand. On the paper is a drawing of a box, and in that box are three stick figures that are supposed to resemble people, with one of those stick people sitting on what looks like wheels. The rest of the paper is covered in pink and purple glitter. She calls glitter 'magic' because the sparkles remind her of the magic in her favorite movie Cinderella.

"It's beautiful, sweetie. Who's that in the box?" I ask her.

With her little finger she points to the smallest figure which is a head with legs. "Dis is me," then points to the one beside it, "dis is you, Momma," which is a slightly bigger head with longer legs, "and dis is Reid." Reid is the head with wheels instead of legs. "Momma, look, we in da magic box dat goes up," she says with a huge smile. The box is the elevator at Reid's that she believes is magic, which explains all the glitter.

"You did a wonderful job, Ava. Are you ready to go home? I mean to Reid's? Let's go grab your lunch box, okay?" I tell her as I take her hand and walk to her cubby. After collecting all her things, we walk out to my car, and I get her buckled into her car seat in the back.

"Momma, guess what?"

"What, baby?"

"Michael ate a booger today. He's nasty. Boys are gross," she enlightens me with her four-year-old gossip of the day, making me laugh as I pull out of the parking lot.

"Ew, that is gross. You're not supposed to eat boogers." I play along with her banter, hoping to get my point across that, in fact, you don't eat boogers.

Laughing, my daughter says, "Dats what I tell him, but he doesn't listen. Maybe his momma did not tell him dat it's gross."

And just like that, a conversation about eating boogers has made the stress of my day fall by the wayside. Pulling up alongside Reid's blue truck, I turn off my car, get out and unload my daughter, who all but runs to the lower entrance door hoping to catch a ride in the magic box. Reid never said I couldn't use this entrance or that we weren't allowed on the elevator, so I walk up to the door where Ava is bouncing from one foot to the other as I punch in the security code. Once locking the door back, we make our way to the lift.

"Can I push the button, Momma?"

Holding my things and balancing Ava on my right hip, I smile and nod my head giving her permission. Pushing the button, we start to rise, and I watch her face light up. Stopping, I open the gate, and we walk out. The first thing Ava does is run down the hall toward our room, no doubt getting the iPad so she can watch a movie while I get dinner going. I don't have much to do since I put a roast with potatoes and carrots in the crockpot this morning, so all I need to do is bake some bread rolls. I walk down the hall heading to my room and find Ava sitting on her bed cross-legged, hugging her Care Bear and watching Moana. "Sweetie, Momma is going to check on Reid. Stay in here and watch your movie until dinner is ready okay?" I bend down kissing her on the top of her head.

"Okay, Momma," she says without taking her eyes off the screen.

She really is a good kid. Sure, she's a typical four-year-old full of energy and questions, but she always listens. I've never had a hard time with her. She's a very smart and independent little girl. Turning, I walk out of mine and Ava's room and head down to the end of the hall toward Reid's.

Knocking on the door, I wait for an answer. Listening, I can hear the faint sounds of the shower running. For a moment, my hand hovers over the door handle, contemplating if I should go in and check on him or not. It's my job, and like it or not, I have to make sure he doesn't need any assistance. Twisting the knob, I walk into his room. Slowing my steps, I round the corner of his dresser that's located right next to his bathroom door, and I find Reid sitting in his wheelchair staring blankly at the floor with the hot water running and steam filling the room. I pause a moment to give him time to realize I'm standing here. When he does, he lifts his gaze to mine. His face is marred by a look of defeat and exhaustion. Closing his eyes, he inhales deeply then lets it out. Aware he may not have enough strength after today's activities to lift himself from his chair into the shower, I decide to step in.

Without a word, I walk over to the cabinet and take out a couple of towels, sitting one on the counter and placing the other one on the wet tiled shower bench to help ensure he doesn't slip. Taking the ponytail holder from my wrist, I pull my long hair up, twisting it into a loose bun. Lucky for me his shower head is one of those that has a detachable center. Reaching in, I adjust the water temperature and angle the spray away, so I don't soak myself.

Stepping back, I look at him. He's been watching my every move but hasn't spoken. I can feel my heart rate pick up. I'm a nurse, I'm about to do my job, but I'm still a woman. A woman who finds the man sitting in front of me very attractive. Pushing that aside, I reach for the hem of his shirt and begin to pull it up exposing his abs. Complying with my movements, he raises his arms enough for me to slip it off his casted arm and over his head. Working with me, he leans, shifting his weight from one side then the other so that I can work his jogging pants over his hips and down his legs. Pulling them completely free of his legs, I reach for his prosthetic. His hand shoots out to stop me. Lifting my eyes to meet his, I silently assure him to trust me. I don't feel words are needed at this moment. Words may do more harm than good. Reid needs to see I only want to help. He needs to feel that he can trust me. Slowly he removes his hold, and I proceed in removing his prosthesis. After removing the compression sock, I stand to leave him in only his black boxers. I won't remove those; I decide to leave them on, not only to help him feel more comfortable but myself as well.

Reid is in excellent shape. He lost a little bit of weight from being in the hospital for a month, but not enough to lose any of his muscle definition. Bending at my knees, I place my arms under his armpits and clasp my hands behind his back to get a secure hold of him. Readying himself, he leans forward, putting his good arm on my shoulder as I hoist him from his chair and onto the towel covered seat. A small grunt leaves my lips. I've done this same maneuver several times since becoming a nurse, but haven't lifted a man of his size before.

Grabbing the showerhead, I keep my eyes trained on his as I wet him down. I'm sure he can take it from here, but a part of me wants to see how far he will trust me to go. I grab the shampoo and squeeze a small amount into my palm and apply it to his hair, keeping eye contact with each other as I gently run my nails along his scalp. Briefly, Reid closes his eyes, relaxing into my touch. When he opens them again, I'm not prepared for the depth of lust I see, and it causes my body to heat as I feel my face start to flush.

When I grab the body wash from the shower caddy, he doesn't stop me. I lather some soap onto the rag. I place the rag on his shoulder, working across to the other and drag the cloth down in a circular motion over his back. Careful to keep his cast dry, I lather one arm before moving to the other. The intimacy of washing him isn't lost on me, and the way his eyes are burning into me with such intensity causes my breathing to falter. Moving to his chest, then down his abs. His breath hitches slightly. Methodically, I make my way down his body. Doing my best, I train my eyes away from his noticeably large arousal straining against his wet boxers and work on washing each leg, taking my time to massage the sore muscles at the same time, which earns a throaty moan from Reid. Once I've finished the process of scrubbing him down, I grab the showerhead and turn back to face him.

"I think I need to take it from here, Kitten," his deep, gravelly voice informs me.

I don't protest and hand him the showerhead. "I'm going to check on Ava. As soon as you get rinsed off, let me know. I'll help you out," I say to him before turning and walking out. I shut the bathroom door behind me, but leave his bedroom door open so that I can hear him. Peaking in on my daughter, I notice her attention is still consumed by the movie she is watching, so I walk back and sit on the edge of Reid's bed and wait.

I can survive taking care of Reid in a purely professional manner. My job depends on it, so there is no question as to the fact that I can and will make sure I perform to the best of my abilities and to the extent he will allow me to. The issue I'm starting to realize is the full effect this man is beginning to have on me as a woman. Sure, I've always been attracted to him, but there, in the shower only moments ago, I felt this pull. I don't need that kind of distraction. If I'm honest with myself, I'm not sure if I'm going to be able to separate the man from the patient.

7

---

## REID

What the hell was I thinking? Between self-pity and being so fuckin' tired and sore from physical therapy earlier today, I couldn't get myself into the shower and checked out. I was aware Mila walked into the bathroom—aware she studied me and never said a word. It piqued my interest in her a little more, which prompted me to keep my mouth shut. When Mila started to undress me, I studied her. I was curious to see how far she would be willing to go for me—to help me.

I shouldn't have found the whole process a turn on either, but I did. It was like she was etching her name into my flesh with every stroke as she washed me. I became hyper-aware of every square inch she touched and the effect it was having on her as well. I became solely focused on her. Her movement. Her breathing. I tried to control my body's reaction to her but failed. The fact she never missed a beat, even after she made her way passed my very noticeable hard-on, and stayed focused on her true intentions wasn't lost on me either. She wasn't only doing her job, but she was also showing—no, she was teaching me to trust her, and it was that revelation that had me stop everything. I wasn't trying to be rude or cruel when I told her to leave. It had to do with the fact I was unprepared for how it made me feel. Managing to gain my self-control after she left, I reach out, turning the water off and grabbing the towel she placed within reach. "Mila!" I call out. "You can come back in."

The door handle turns, and slowly she opens the door stepping in. "Would you like help to get back into your chair?" she asks.

"Please, I'm wiped out, so if you can help, that would be great. I can take it from there once I'm out of the shower." Walking up, she grabs another towel from the cabinet, placing it on the seat of the wheelchair before helping me, and as skillfully as before she gets me back in my chair.

"You sure you don't need any help dressing or getting into bed? It's what I'm here for. To help," she affirms.

"No." I rub the back of my head with my hand. "I can handle it."

Mila gives a small smile, and a nod then walks out of the bathroom. The click of my bedroom door lets me know she has left. Soon after, I wheel myself over to my dresser and gather some clothes from the drawers. The task of getting myself onto the bed was no big deal, but peeling damp boxers off my body with one hand is.

Physical therapy kicked my ass today. Getting up and back down from a seated position with assistance was what I went through today. The back pain I can handle. It's the muscle fatigue and cramps from the lack of use that's killin' me right now. The deep muscle massage Mila gave my legs in the shower did wonders to soothe the ache I was feeling from putting weight on them.

Once I've tackled the task of getting dressed, I contemplate whether to grab some dinner or go straight to bed. I know Mila has prepared a roast because I've smelled it cooking in the crockpot in the kitchen most of the day. I venture out toward the kitchen and find her and Ava sitting at the table.

"Oh, hey." Mila looks up from placing her daughter's plate of food in front of her. "Would you like to join us or take your food to your office?"

I have been held up in my room or my office since I've been home. Partly avoiding her, but mostly trying to bury myself in work-related tasks since I'm useless anywhere else instead of in front of a computer screen now. "I'll eat at the table," I tell her as I push one of the chairs to the side and position the wheelchair in its place.

"Momma, Momma, can I give it to him now?" Ava starts bouncing in her seat. Mila turns from preparing my plate and heads toward the table, placing it in front of me with a fork and a glass of water. What I want is a cold beer. "Thanks," I reply.

"Ava, sit down. Let Reid eat, then you can give him the picture," she tells her daughter.

"Pwease, Momma?" she tries once again, but this time she adds puppy eyes. You can see a little of Mila in her appearance, but I'm guessing she looks a lot more like her father. I've always been a bit curious as to what that whole situation is about. Where is he? He isn't in their lives, or at least he doesn't appear to be. I don't know her well enough to make that assumption. Before she sits, she places her plate on the table and turns to face me. "Um, Ava drew a picture in preschool today and has insisted you have it. Would it be okay if she gives it to you now?" she asks looking exhausted.

Looking over at her daughter, I watch her squirm in her seat, waiting for the answer she's looking for. The anticipation and excitement in her blue eyes are too much for me to say no to. I sit back in my chair and ask Ava, "Whatcha got kid?"

Reaching over, she grabs a piece of paper that was sitting in the seat beside her and slides out of her chair. The damn paper is covered in so much glitter some falls from the page, leaving a light dusted trail on the floor as she makes her way around to me.

Holding it up for me to see, she begins to explain what I'm looking at. "Dis is me cuz I'm wittle," Ava explains pointing her little finger to a small blob on the picture. "And dis one here is my momma." Next, she points to a square with wheels. "And dis is you and your wheelchair. We are riding in the elwavater." After giving the details of her creation, Ava then hands me the picture with a proud look on her face.

I stare at the picture, not knowing what to say, but it makes me smile. I run my hand through my hair as Ava skips back over to her seat, and Mila gets her situated again before sitting down herself. "Thank you, Ava. It's a beautiful picture." I clear my throat and place it down on the table beside me. "Maybe your momma can put it on the refrigerator for me later," I mumble, looking down at my food as I pick up a bite with my fork.

Giggling, Ava starts to eat. I look over at Mila to find her staring at me. "What?"

"Nothing. By the way, you have some glitter in your hair," she smirks. A laughing Ava chimes in, "You have magic in your hair. It's so pretty! Momma, I want magic in my hair, too," she chatters.

"Why don't we all eat before it gets cold," Mila announces.

The rest of the meal is eaten in silence, both Mila and I stealing glances at one another. When Ava is through, Mila excuses herself to bathe and put her daughter to bed. The least I can do is clean up the kitchen. Once I have the leftovers in the fridge and dishwasher loaded, I make my way back to my room for the night.

Now, I'm lying here in my bed a few hours later, and Mila is all I can think about. Falling for a woman like her, smart, driven, caring, sassy, and sexy as fuck would be so damn easy. The thought alone of her long black hair wrapped around my fist as she wraps those plump, pouty lips around my cock has me wanting to throw all caution out the window. She stirs things in me I don't want to feel. That woman would be the fall of any man lucky enough to have her. I'm afraid if I allow myself one taste of Mila, she would be the end of me.

———————

"COME ON, *you have to admit that little bombshell in the teacher get up was fuckin' hot," I tell my brother while we head back home from the clubhouse. Tomorrow he leaves for college, so the club decided to throw him a going away party. Quinn went all out with the girls tonight too. A redhead dressed as little red riding hood, a sexy fuckin' nurse, and a black-haired beauty with huge-ass tits dressed as a naughty school teacher.*

*"Yeah, those were hard to ignore when she shoved them in my face. Quinn outdid himself. You'll have to thank him for me," he laughs.*

*Normally, my ass would be on my bike leadin' the way home, but I got a tad carried away tonight, so my brother is driving us home. Shifting my weight, I twist my body to look at my brother. "Noah. All shittin' aside. I'm fuckin' proud of you. I've always known that brain of yours would get you places," I admit to him.*

*"I'm gonna miss you, Reid. I'll even miss the rest of the family. The club—They're my brothers too."*

*"Fuck, California isn't that far away. I'll be comin' to visit every chance I can get."*

*No sooner does my brother's face break into a smile when a large eighteen-wheeler veers into our lane, headlights blinding my vision. Noah tries to avoid the impact, but instantly the sounds of crunching glass and twisting metal encapsulate me. My ears are ringing, and pain is radiating through the lower half of my body. The sounds of moans and smells of gasoline and smoke fill the air around me. I reach my hand out, desperately grasping for Noah, finally finding his hand. I look at him and try to focus through my dazed vision, and that's when I see it. A* metal rod coming through the shattered windshield impaled straight into Noah's chest. *Panic sets in and my fight instincts kick into high gear, yet I can't move to help him. "Noah, stay with me.* **Noah!***" I roar.*

I shoot straight up in bed, the tail end of Noah's name leaving my lips as beads of sweat drip down my forehead. *What the hell?* I haven't dreamt of that night in over a year. I scrub my hand down my face and glance at the alarm clock sitting on my nightstand. 5:00 am. Well, I'm wide awake now. Getting out of bed, I take myself to the kitchen and start some coffee, careful to be quiet.

With my coffee in hand, I make my way into the elevator and head down to my office. I might as well get started on some paperwork. I need to sort through some new job applicants today. When Nikolai and the club went into a business partnership several months ago and started a construction company, we mostly wanted to specialize in industrial and architectural builds. So far, the demands have been steady, and bids have been in our favor. We even landed a pretty lucrative job while I was laid up in the hospital. Nikolai and Prez handled shit while I was out of commission, which was a shit ton of paperwork and red tape. A very prominent businessman by the name of Declan O'Connell wants to build a sizable mountain resort between here and Bozeman. This deal is enormous and will provide people in the community with jobs.

An hour later, I'm still sifting through the applicants when I get a call from Nikolai. Picking my phone up from the desktop, I swipe the screen. "Hey, man. What's up?"

"Reid, how are you today, my friend? You sound tired. You ready to go over the final contract that was faxed over to you from O'Connell's people yesterday?"

I reach over and pick up the file containing the contract mentioned. I haven't had time to look it over, so getting Nikolai to swing by and us going over it together would kill two birds with one stone. "Yeah, listen, do you have time to swing by this morning? Let's both go over the fine details together and see if we can get all the final signatures on the dotted line by the end of the day."

"Okay, sounds good. I can be there in a couple of hours. Say, 8:00 am?" he says in his thick Russian accent.

"Alright, I'll see you then," I reply. Before sitting the phone back down, I tap into the camera feed upstairs that allows me to see the kitchen and living room areas. The only places in my home that don't have surveillance are the bedrooms and of course, the bathrooms. As soon as the app opens, I see Mila in the living room on the couch with a cup of coffee, sitting quietly by herself watching the morning news report on the TV.

I sit and watch her for several minutes as she enjoys a moment alone—well, almost alone —before closing the app and sitting my phone down. I need to get her out of my head.

Determined to do just that, I fire up the rest of my systems and start digging into the backgrounds of some of these applicants before Nikolai gets here.

# 8

## MILA

When I woke up this morning, Reid was already up and in his office downstairs, and after last night's events, I decided against going down to check on him. That and the fact that I wasn't allowed in his office. I opted to send him a quick text asking if he needed anything before I took Ava to preschool. He replied the same way he usually did.

**Me:** *Need anything before I take Ava to preschool*

**Reid:** *No*

With a frustrated breath, I go to slip my phone in my purse only to stop when it pings with another text.

**Reid:** Thank you

THANK YOU? I stare down at my phone and can't help but smile. The shift in his attitude is welcome. So, I reply.

**Me:** *You're welcome*

---

HEARING THE DOORBELL, I look up from the stove where I'm cooking Reid his breakfast. I don't bother answering. I know Reid saw whoever it is before they were at the door. Seconds later, Nikolai walks through the door. Nikolai is Logan's brother. Their looks are very similar; only he has black hair and not brown. The trait that stands out the most is his eyes. Nikolai and Logan both have one green eye and one blue, just like their father. I watch as he comes striding in. He's wearing old faded jeans and a black t-shirt paired with boots. Typical attire for someone who works in construction. I prefer a guy who works with his hands over a polished suit and tie kind of man. But looking at Nikolai, I realize even though I find him attractive, he does absolutely nothing for me. Not like the grumpy ass biker downstairs. Walking into the kitchen, he helps himself to some coffee before casually leaning against the counter. "How are you doing today, Krasavitsa *beautiful*"? he asks.

"I'm doing okay, how about yourself?" I return and mentally remind myself to look up what Krasavitsa means. I haven't been around Nikolai much, only when Bella has invited me over to the clubhouse for family gatherings. He's always sweet and respectful. Just when he opens his mouth and is about to respond, a loud booming voice comes over the intercom. "Nikolai, get your ass downstairs." That voice is Reid's. I still haven't gotten used to all the cameras Reid has in and around his home. And I know he is watching us this very moment.

With a warm smile, Nikolai places his coffee mug in the sink. "I better get my ass down there. It was good seeing you, Mila."

"You too," I return.

Just as he goes to turn away, I call out to him, "Would you mind taking Reid's breakfast down to him since you're heading that way?" I ask, picking up a serving tray with a plate of scrambled eggs, sausage, and toast, along with some orange juice.

"No problem, Krasavitsa *beautiful*."

"Thanks."

After stripping the sheets off Reid's bed and starting a load of laundry, I go about cleaning the bathroom, sweeping, mopping the floors and washing the dirty dishes from breakfast. Before I know it, two hours have passed, and I haven't seen Nikolai come back up from downstairs. When I look out the window, I see his car is gone. He must have left from the ground entrance. Since it seems like Reid is going to spend most of the day working, I decide to visit my Grams. Once I'm finished preparing lunch for Reid, I place it in the microwave. That way, all he has to do is warm it up. I pick my phone up off the counter to send a text to Reid, then quickly decide I'm tired of texting him when we need to communicate. We're in the same damn house for Christ's sake. I know his office is off limits, but the texting is ridiculous. Walking over to the front door, I pick up my keys and purse. Tossing my phone into my bag and slinging it over my shoulder, I proceed to make my way down to Reid's office. When I make it to his office, the door is closed. The only sound I hear is the clicking coming from him typing away on his computer. Without a second thought, I knock.

"Come in!" Reid calls out.

Opening the door, I see him sitting behind a desk. Looking up from his work, Reid regards me. "I'm going to go see my grandmother. I won't be gone long. Your lunch is in the microwave. And I know you said your office is off limits, but it's ridiculous to have to text you when we are in the same house," I finish, sounding a little exasperated. When I'm done, I notice Reid looks a tad amused at my frustration.

"You're welcome to come down here anytime, Kitten. The day I said that I was having a bad day." Not knowing what else to say, I nod my head and go to shut the door when he stops me.

"Mila?"

Lifting my gaze, I look at him, "Yes?"

"I'm glad you're here."

I nod my head once again before closing the door because what do I say to that? Reid's attitude has done a complete turn-around. And men say women are confusing.

I'm walking down the hall of the nursing home toward my grandmother's room when I hear several raised voices. One of them I recognize as Grams. She sounds frantic and scared, and that has me picking up my pace. After getting closer to her room, I recognize another voice. It's been four years since I've laid eyes on her. Rushing into my grandmother's room, I come face to face with my mother and standing on the opposite side of the room, my father.

*What in the hell are they doing here?*

Ignoring my parents, I rush over to my grandmother and the nurse, who is trying to calm her down. My grandmother is hysterical, and she keeps repeating the words, "Leave her alone! Leave her alone! You can't have it!"

*Can't have what?*

I hate this disease. It breaks my heart, seeing my grandmother like this. She gets so confused sometimes and works herself into hysterics. And the sudden appearance by my parents has no doubt triggered her current reaction. Feeling my blood boil, I turn away from my grandmother and come face to face with my mother again. "You need to leave **now**," I demand through gritted teeth, ignoring the fact that this is the first time I have seen or spoken to her in four years. Nothing about my mother has changed. She is still the same polished and put together woman she was the last time I saw her in my hospital room after giving birth to Ava.

"I think you have forgotten who you're speaking to," she snaps, narrowing her eyes at me.

"Oh, trust me, mother; I know exactly who I'm talking to. Now, I will say it one more time. Get the hell out of this room before I have security remove you." I enunciate each word. Just when she's about to argue my father cuts in.

"Come on, Susan. Nothing more can be done right now. Not when she's in this state."

*What is he talking about?*

Huffing, my mother turns and walks out of the room alongside my father. I don't give them a second glance. Instead, I turn my attention back to my grandmother, who has suddenly stopped fighting the nurse. "Come on, Grams, let's get you back in bed, okay?"

Once we get her settled back into bed, I can tell the fight she just gave us has worn her out. I turn toward the nurse, "She's okay now. I'll stay with her until she falls asleep. Can you please alert the staff that those two people are not allowed back in here? I'll sign whatever paperwork is necessary before I leave."

After the nurse has left, I pull a chair up close to the bed and take my grandmother's trembling hand in mine as I begin to stroke her hair. Several minutes later, her eyes close, and her breaths even out. Her good days are coming fewer and farther between. I want more than anything to walk in here one day and have my old Grams back, but the reality is that is never going to happen. Some days when I visit, there are brief moments when she looks at me, and I see her, the real her, and she'll smile at me, but then as quickly as those moments come, they soon vanish. One thing I know for sure, I will not let this disease take away who my grandmother is and how I will remember her because she lives inside of me. I am the woman and mother I am because of her.

I'm on my way back to Reid's after stopping and picking Ava up from preschool and my mind is reeling from today's events. When I left my grandmother's room, my parents were already gone. The nurse at the nurse's station informed me they tried to access her medical records but were denied. I am her appointed Power of Attorney; they would need my permission. The nurse said they left after a brief argument. I bet my mother just loved that, she hates to be told no. I let out a snort and shake my head at the vision of my mother in all her sophisticated snobbery as she demanded a nurse break the law and hand over Gram's file. Knowing my parents, that is exactly what they thought was going to happen. It's ridiculous when you think about it, considering they are both lawyers. My parents are very well known and respected in New York, but Polson is a far cry from the big city, and people here don't have a clue who Richard and Susan Vaughn is.

Now my biggest question is, what do they want? Why show up after so many years? Even growing up, my mother never came to visit Grams. And I'm pretty sure the only calls she received from my mom was when she needed a place to dump me during the summers. I have a nagging feeling in the pit of my stomach that my parents are up to no good. No way is my mother here out of the goodness of her heart or out of love. Richard and Susan Vaughn don't know the meaning of the word. The only people they look out for are themselves. Always have, always will. Something is up with them; I just need to figure out what and keep them away from Grams in the process. I refuse to have what went down today happen again.

I abandon my thoughts as I pull up in front of Reid's place. Unbuckling, I turn to look in the back seat to see my little girl fast asleep. A pang of sadness washes over me when taking in her blonde curls that partially cover her face. She looks so much like him. I'm sad she will never know her father. I want to think he would have made a fantastic dad. Ava asked me once why she didn't have a daddy like the kids at preschool. I told her she had a daddy, but he went to heaven when she was still in my tummy. I don't even have a picture of him, but I don't need one because all I need to do is look at Ava, and I see him.

A loud rapping on my driver's side window brings me out of my fog and causes me to jump. Looking to my left, I see Reid at my window. With my hand still clutched to my chest, I let my window down.

"Sorry, babe. Didn't mean to scare ya. You've been sittin' out here for a while, and I wanted to see if you were okay."

Closing my eyes, I try to get my rapidly beating heart under control. When I reopen them, I'm met with Reid's green ones. Lord, this man is gorgeous. Even with his disheveled hair and a week's worth of stubble on his face, he's still a sight.

After a few moments, I'm able to find my voice. "Yeah, I'm fine. Ava fell asleep on the way home, and I didn't want to disturb her just yet. That and it's been a long day. I needed a breather myself." With a look of understanding on his face, Reid gives me a slight nod before he moves his chair over to the back passenger door of my car, then proceeds to open it. I watch as he leans in, unbuckles Ava from her car seat, hoists her out and brings her to his chest. Once she is securely in the grasp of his casted right arm, he shuts the car door. The whole time my daughter never rouses from her sleep.

"You comin'?" Reid questions over his shoulder as he makes his way inside. Meanwhile, I'm still sitting in my car with a shocked expression, telling myself not to let the sight in front of me go to my head. There is a reason I stay away from getting involved with a man and not let myself get swept up in silly moments like this one, and that reason is my daughter. Ava is my number one priority, and my grandmother is my second. Being here is just another job—nothing more. Besides, Reid is only being kind, and it would be silly of me to go gaga seeing him holding my little girl. Like how he picked Ava up and carried her close like it was something he did every day. Nope, not going to let it get to me. *Liar.*

Sucking in a deep breath, I grab my purse from the seat beside me and step out of my car. "What have you gotten yourself into,

Mila?" I mutter to myself. I wouldn't have a single clue what I would do with a man like Reid.

When I got pregnant with Ava, I was only nineteen. That was almost five years ago. It was also the only time I have been with a guy. The night I spent with Ava's father was my attempt to let go and be free even if for just a moment. But look where that got me. Pregnant at nineteen. Not that I regret my decision. I have never regretted having my daughter. She is the best thing to ever happen to me. But I've learned what hardships come from the choices we make. I can't let myself slip ever again.

Later that night, after putting Ava to bed, I'm standing at the kitchen sink washing dishes and staring out the window in front of me lost in thought. Thinking about my parents being in town still has me on edge. I can't shake the feeling that something terrible is coming.

"Want some help, Kitten?" Reid's deep voice asks from behind me.

Startled, I whip around, and the glass in my hand slips from my grip, falling to the floor and shatters into dozens of little pieces. "Shit! I'm so sorry," I rush to say as I bend down and start picking the glass off the floor. "I'll buy you a new one. I promise I'm not usually this jumpy," I explain.

"Mila?" Reid calls out my name.

Looking up at him from my crouched position on the floor, I see he has a look of concern on his face. "It's just a glass, babe. It's not a big deal."

As I use a broom to sweep up my mess, Reid not once takes his eyes off me. His intense stare causes my skin to prickle and my hands to shake. *Why is he just sitting there watching me?* After the glass is cleaned up, I go to walk past him to the sink to finish my task when he reaches out and grabs hold of my wrist. Swallowing past the lump in my throat, I look to Reid and wait for him to speak.

"You want to talk about what has you on edge? Is it me? Am I doin' something to make you uncomfortable?"

His last question makes me quick to react. Does he think he was making me feel uncomfortable? "What? No! Reid, nothing about being here with you is uncomfortable. A little weird? Yes. But uncomfortable? Never," I affirm, looking him straight in his eyes so that he can see my sincerity.

Reid studies my face for a minute. Satisfied with what he sees, he continues, "You want to tell me what's got you so upset then?"

Waving my hand in attempts to play off my frazzled state today, I reply, "It's nothing really, just some family stuff. I'm sure everything will be fine." At my last statement, I go to step away from him, but he refuses to release his hold on me.

"Is it your grandmother? Is she alright?" His show of concern for my Grams warms my heart.

"Yeah, Grams is okay. As good as to be expected anyway. Seriously, I'm fine," I lie. By the look on Reid's face, he knows it, and by the grip he still has on my wrist, I don't think he is willing to let it go.

## 9

### REID

I stare at a frazzled, worn out looking Mila as she sits on the sofa while I wait for her to speak. Moments ago, she was standing at the kitchen sink washing dishes so lost in thought; she didn't even hear me when I was behind her calling her name. She had been washing the glass in her hand for the past ten minutes. I could tell something was bothering her, but what?

Mila startles when she finally realizes she was not alone, causing her to drop the glass she was holding, and I watched as it shattered all over the kitchen floor. I didn't say anything for a few moments. I let her go about cleaning up the mess, and I listened to her ramble off an apology and something about replacing the glass she accidentally broke. Seeing her so upset had me feeling a sudden need to comfort her.

Then I started to think maybe me being an asshole was the cause of her current state. After I questioned her about my suspicions, she quickly denied her nervous state had anything to do with me. Mila admitted she was having family issues. Again, with this overwhelming need to help her, I level her with a stare encouraging her to open up to me.

In the short amount of time I've spent with Mila, one thing I know for sure about this woman is that she is incredibly strong. I sense that she is used to handling matters on her own. Mila is very good at putting up a front. She has a wall built up around herself, and everything in me wants to tear it down. I want to know everything about her. I wish Mila would trust me enough to give a piece of herself to me. Holding onto her wrist, I patiently wait to see if she would give in; if she is willing to provide me with something, anything.

The rage and jealousy I felt this morning when I saw Nikolai standing in the kitchen talking to Mila sent me into a tailspin. I've never gotten jealous over a woman before. I wanted to rip Nikolai's head off. Of course, when he came into my office, he had to give me shit. But it was his words which pissed me off.

"If you're not going to pursue Mila, I have it in mind to ask her out," he stated.

"Unless you want me to put a bullet in your ass, you better back off," I warned him.

After studying me for a moment, Nikolai responded with a slight bow of his head, "Duly noted."

Satisfied with his response, we went on to discussing business. I knew Nikolai was serious about asking Mila out. If it were Quinn talking, I'd know it would be him fucking with me. Unlike my brother, Nikolai isn't a jokester. And for that reason alone, if I don't want someone to come in and sweep this incredible woman out from under my nose, then I need to act. I need to take what I want. It's time for me to quit acting like a jackass. That would be my first step. The second step is for me to gain her trust. With Mila, I feel this will be the biggest challenge.

I don't know anything about her past, but I have a feeling she doesn't trust easily. The only close person Mila has in her life is her grandmother, so I am going to assume her issues lie with her parents or Ava's father. The thought of a man doing something to hurt this beautiful woman instantly has my blood boiling. *Fuck.* What if that's what she meant by family problems? Is it Ava's dad? Is he in the picture? Did he leave them, and now he wants them back? *Hell fuckin' no, that shit's not happening.* How could any man leave a woman like Mila? And Ava. That little girl has done something to my heart, and she did it all with a damn picture. So, that brings me to the third thing that needs to be done, and that is for me to push myself and work hard to get better, to get myself out of this chair, to become the man I need to be. I want Mila. And that means getting off my ass and going after what I want.

"Reid, are you okay?" Mila asks, placing her hand on my arm, bringing me back to the present. When I see the concerned look on her face, I realize my body has gone tense, and my fists are clenched. "Yeah, babe, I'm good. How about you tell me what's going on?" Nodding and licking her lips, Mila moves her hand off my arm, and I instantly miss her touch.

"I went to visit my grandmother today, and my parents were there." When she doesn't continue, I give her a perplexed look. "Okay, and is that a problem?" I ask.

She narrows her eyes, "Yes, considering my parents haven't had anything to do with me or my grandmother in four years, I'd say that's a huge problem. I'm talking, no visits, no phone calls, not even a goddamn postcard. Nothing," Mila finishes. Standing up from the sofa, she begins to pace the living room. "I mean what the hell could they possibly want? They don't care about Grams, and they damned sure don't give a shit about Ava or me. They made it pretty clear almost five years ago when they told me to either have an abortion or give my daughter up!" Mila nearly shouts as she flails her arm around. Her admission catches me off guard.

"What the fuck do you mean give your daughter up? They told you to choose abortion or adoption?" I seethe.

Turning her attention back to me, I see the look of disgust and sadness on Mila's face, "I was on the fast track to Harvard Law when I became pregnant with Ava," Mila confesses, looking down as if she is ashamed to have revealed that bit of information to me.

Not wanting her to feel any more uncomfortable, I keep the conversation going. "Let me guess, going to law school was your parents' idea, and you getting pregnant hindered their plans for you?"

Walking back over to the couch, Mila sits down and lets out an exasperated breath. "You got it. No way would Richard, or Susan Vaughn accept their only child not going to college. Both of my parents are well known and highly respected attorneys in New York. As their daughter, I was expected to follow in their footsteps. They even wanted me to marry the son of one of the partners in their firm. They had my whole life mapped out for me. One summer, I spent time with Grams and I wanted for once to throw caution to the wind. Growing up, I never had many friends. I never went out; I didn't date. I didn't go to parties. My sole focus was on school. To be the best, to have the best grades. I was trying to make my parents proud. To make them, I don't know..." Mila pauses.

"Love you," I finish for her. She raises her head, and when her eyes meet mine, I see hers well up with tears before one escapes down her cheek. I reach out and grab her hand, then pull her toward me. Without protest, Mila slides onto my lap, and I pull her into my chest and wrap my arms around her. No more words are spoken as I allow this beautiful and incredibly brave woman to cry. She cries for the childhood she deserved but didn't get. She cries for the fact her parents didn't love her. And Mila cries for the little girl sleeping down the hall. The daughter she chose to sacrifice everything for.

I don't know how much time has passed before Mila's cries turn into sobs. Eventually, her body relaxes, and her breaths even out. I don't dare move her. I sit in the living room for hours as I continue to hold her. It's then that I decide what I'm going to do. First thing tomorrow, I am going to find out who the fuck Richard and Susan Vaughn are and why the hell they have crashed back into Mila's life. Because she's right, something is not adding up.

# 10

## MILA

A few weeks have gone by, and everyone has fallen into a comfortable routine. Every day Reid can do more on his own, and at every one of his therapy sessions, he has progressed faster than doctors anticipated. He has days when being in his chair frustrates him more than others. Take Alba and Gabriel's wedding for example. He was having a hard time maneuvering across the yard and snapped at me when I tried helping him out. He later apologized. I need to remember a man's pride is everything to him. Especially a man like Reid. He didn't like looking vulnerable in front of his brothers.

The swelling around his spinal cord has reduced significantly, and in turn, they've been able to determine in time he should regain complete function and feeling in both his legs that he had before the most recent accident. I'll be sad to go when he no longer needs me. I've become very fond of him. We've both been dancing around unspoken attraction for one another since before I started this assignment.

Ava has become very attached to Reid since our stay here in his home. As soon as she gets up in the mornings, she is looking for him or calling his name. As soon as she's home from preschool, it's the same thing all over again. I won't say she'll be the only one to miss him; I know I will too.

Weeks ago, I poured some of my heart out to him, not too much, just what was weighing me down at the time. The whole situation with my parents and Grams had me on edge. I wasn't looking to dump my worries on someone, but I instinctively felt like I could trust Reid with a little piece of me. When he pulled me into his lap that night and let me cry, let me release a portion of what I had been keeping bottled up for years, he showed me compassion.

It's crazy how fast it all happened, but I think I'm falling for Reid Carter, and it scares me. Besides Grams, the only person I know I can count on in my life is myself. What if he does like me in return? What if we did start a relationship? What if it doesn't work out if we try? I couldn't put Ava through heartache like that, especially when she adores him so much already, and what about my heart? I'm not sure I'm willing to hand it over to someone who, as of right now, has so much of a hold on it as it is.

This morning Reid finally got his cast taken off his arm. And after going through several rehab sessions of physical therapy for the past few weeks, I'm watching him walk out of the Doctor's office this afternoon using crutches, which means my time with him will be over soon, and I think we both realize what that means. At least I know what it means to me. "It's about time for me to pick Ava up from preschool. Mind if we swing by on the way back to your place?" I ask him as we make our way to the car.

He makes his way around to the driver's side before I open the door, "Not a problem." He reaches for the door handle.

"What are you doing?"

"Doctor said I could start driving again, so I'm drivin', babe. Go get your sweet ass in the passenger's seat," he informs me. Sticking his hand out, he waits for me to hand over my car keys. Digging into my purse, I take out the keys and hand them over.

Once we make it to the preschool center, Reid pulls up in front of the entrance instead of parking in a parking spot. "I'll wait right here for ya, babe."

"I won't be but a minute." I smile. I'm a few minutes earlier than usual, so when I get to Ava's class, I find all the little ones busy picking up toys and putting them back into the places they belong and overhear my daughter having a conversation with her best friend, a little-redheaded girl named Willow.

"My daddy said I could bring a friend to my party," she tells my daughter eagerly.

"Weally? I wanna go. Can I go too?"

Did she get invited to a birthday party I don't know about?

"Hey, munchkin," a deep voice I recognize from behind me calls out, and Willow giggles then runs past me. I turn around to see her dad, River reaching for his daughter. "Hey, Mila. How have you been? I haven't seen you around for awhile. How's your Grams?" he inquires.

River lives down the road from Grams' house. He moved in about a year ago. He's a widower. He lost his wife while giving birth to their daughter. Willow and Ava get along so well that I sometimes drop her off to play on the weekends. Especially when I was taking night classes during nursing school. River is a good-looking guy. Tall, dark brown hair and grey eyes. From the pictures I've seen, Willow is the spitting image of her mother minus the grey eyes she got from her father.

"Grams is doing okay. I've been helping a friend lately, which is why I haven't been home," I tell him.

"Momma, Willow says I can go to a party." Ava tugs at the pant leg of my scrubs.

"It's not a party. I told Willow on her birthday I would take her

CRYSTAL DANIELS & SANDY ALVAREZ

and a friend to the bounce house downtown. She instantly started asking for Ava," River says.

"Sounds like fun. Give me a day and time, and I'll make sure she's there," I tell him. Happy with what they hear, both girls get the giggles and hug one another.

"Well, I have to get going. You ready, Ava?" I announce.

Running to her cubby, she grabs her coat and lunchbox, then skips her way back over and takes hold of my hand.

"Willow and I will walk you out," River says as he hoists his daughter into his arms.

We walk out of the building, and right away, Ava sees Reid sitting behind the wheel. "Reid!" she squeals with delight.

"This the friend?" River questions with a raised eyebrow.

"It's not like that." I roll my eyes then notice a blonde partially bent over talking with Reid on the driver side. Hearing Ava's laughter causes the woman to stand and glance in our direction over the top of my car.

*Claire.*

I shoot daggers in her direction as anger starts to bubble inside me.

"Oh, hello, Mila," she says with way too much perkiness.

"Are you trying to convince yourself or me?" River says, observing my reaction to the scene in front of us.

*Am I that obvious?*

When Reid turns his head, he sees River standing beside me. The neutral expression he had is gone and replaced with one of anger. Jesus, what a pair we are, both of us staking claim to someone that doesn't belong to us.

"Listen, send me a text about the birthday. We'll be there." I smile as I open the back door, and Ava climbs into her car seat, waiting for me to buckle her in. I watch as Claire bends down to say something to Reid before she looks at me, waves, and makes her way through the preschool doors.

"Say goodbye, Willow," River says, still holding his daughter.

"Bye, Ava." She waves.

"Bye, Willow," Ava replies with a wave of her own.

I toss her things into the back seat and get her buckled in.

Reid tears his eyes away from me and puts the car in drive, gripping the steering wheel the whole ride home. I sit in my seat, stewing in my jealousy as Ava sits in the backseat singing the *Let It Go* song. The irony is not lost on me.

IT'S AFTER DINNER, and Ava has been bathed and put to bed for the night, so I sit down on the couch and start to fill out my paperwork. I'll be going home tomorrow, and Reid finally gets to transition back into having his space again.

"Hey," Reid says from behind me.

"How can you be so quiet on a pair of crutches? That's a little unnerving." I lean my head back and look up at him as he hovers above me from where he is standing. Moving around the corner of the couch, he sits his crutches to the side and situates himself on the sofa.

He's wearing a pair of sweats that are hanging low on his hips, and my gaze drops.

I look up after gazing at his body to find him watching me. Oh god, he caught me looking at his package. Shifting, I squeeze my legs together, trying to suppress the sudden ache I'm feeling between them for this man; trying to ignore the sudden surge of attraction filling the room, I mention the subject we both have been avoiding. "Tonight is mine and Ava's last night here. I'll be heading back home tomorrow. I need to thank you for making us feel welcomed this past month. Ava is going to miss you, so maybe we could drop by for a visit sometime? That's if you're not too busy. I know now that the doctor has cleared you for more activities you'll get back to being busy with work and of course the club," I tell him as the heat starts to rise up my neck, and I feel my cheeks flush because of the way he's looking at me.

Reid twists his body, putting one leg near the back edge of the cushions and leaves the other draped over the side with his foot planted on the floor.

"Come here, Kitten," he orders in a deep voice. Reaching out, he grabs my hand, pulling me toward him. At the moment, I don't question what he's doing or reason with myself as to why I'm complying. I don't think at all. I let what I'm feeling guide me. He pulls me forward until he has my body laid out to where I'm chest to chest with him, and my hips have settled between his legs. My rapidly beating heart feels like it's about to burst from my chest as his eyes drop to my lips. If the hard length I feel pressed against my stomach is any indication, I would say his body is wanting the same as mine.

One taste before I leave tomorrow won't hurt. Will it? I want to know what it feels like to have Reid's lips pressed hard against mine.

"Momma, Momma!" Ava cries out. And just like that, the moment is over. The charge in the atmosphere is so thick, I find it hard to breathe, but the climactic moment I feel we were about to have is suddenly pushed to the side.

I look at him, knowing we both want this to happen, but neither one prepared to say it.

"Momma!" Ava hollers again.

Too wordless to say anything, I get up off the couch and head toward the hall in the direction of mine and Ava's room. "Reid..." I turn to find him watching me walk away, the same look of want in his eyes, and I smile at him. "Goodnight."

With a heavy sigh and a look of understanding, knowing my daughter comes first, he replies, "Goodnight, Kitten."

"WELL, that's it. We are all packed and ready to go, sweetie. Did you remember to grab teddy from your bed?" I say to my daughter as I zip the last suitcase closed. Teddy is her stuffed bear she has had since the day she was born. Grams gave it to her as a welcome home present when we stepped off the bus. She can't sleep without it.

"I got it, Momma," she responds in a sad little whisper.

I know she doesn't want to go, but this was only temporary. Unfortunately, she's too young to understand that right now. "Come on." I kneel and tickle her tummy, trying to steal a smile from her. "We can always visit," I tell her. Looking up, I see Reid standing in the doorway.

"Quinn is here to follow you home since it's getting late."

No sooner does he say his name, than Quinn appears in the hallway behind Reid. "Holy shit, these tacos are good," he says stuffing the last bite of what we had for dinner in his mouth. I watch Ava walk toward the door, squeeze past Reid and his crutches and stop in front of Quinn. I try to hold back a smile because my little girl is on a mission.

She cranes her neck to peer up at him, and he looks down at her with a grin. "What's up little bit?"

All business, Ava puts her hand on her hip and sticks the other one out and voices, "You say a bad word."

"Shit... I mean darn. I'm sorry. Here." He pulls out his wallet and gives her two one-dollar bills. I told him the first time that he made a mistake giving her money like that. Her sass doesn't seem to faze him at all. His smile only gets bigger.

Reid turns from the little chastising Quinn just received from a four-year-old and says to me, "You sure you don't want to head out in the morning?"

"No, I'm all packed and ready to go. Besides, it's not too late. The sun hasn't even set yet," I explain. I should have left sooner, but I wanted to make sure I had prepared a few extra meals for him before I went. He nods his head and starts to make his way down the hall with Ava on his heels and me following behind. Quinn soon follows with our bags in his hands, and we all pile into the lift. Making our way outside to my car, Quinn loads my things and announces he'll wait for me on his bike and walks off lighting a cigarette.

Clearing his throat, Reid speaks, "Listen, the guys are throwing a party for me this weekend. Why don't you and Ava come out to the clubhouse?"

Assuming it's going to be a family-friendly event, or he wouldn't have asked, I decide there isn't any reason to say no. I've been to a few with Bella and have enjoyed myself. Ava made a few friends with some of the members' kids also. "Sure, I'd like that." I smile at him.

Before we turn so I can load Ava into her seat, she pulls away from my grasp and walks to Reid and holds her teddy up. Reid takes it from her tiny outreach hands. "He makes me feel better when I am sad," she warmly says to him. I watch him take in my sweet girl. This is a big gesture from her. I hope he is aware of the fact she is handing him a huge source of comfort. Doing my best not to cry, I silently watch her make a very grown-up decision as her hands let go of her teddy bear.

Squatting, he holds the bear close to him. "Are you sure?"

"I'm sure," she confirms, and my heart swells even more.

"I'll take really good care of him. I promise," he assures her, then wraps her in his arms for a big bear hug. Running back to me, Ava climbs into her car seat. As I'm buckling her in, I lean in and kiss her forehead. "You are such a brave and caring girl, Ava Marie Vaughn."

Rounding the trunk of my car, I glance at Reid, who's now standing and watching. "I'll call when I get settled."

I make it home in fifteen minutes. Quinn carries my suitcases inside and sets them down just inside the living room. "I hate to run, but the guys need me out at the clubhouse. Don't forget to call Reid," he informs me.

"I'll call him soon. Thanks, Quinn."

"Ya know, he didn't want you to leave. Sometimes we gotta take the chance and go all in even when it scares the shit out of us," he says, walking toward the door. "See ya this weekend." Closing the door behind him, I wait and listen for his motorcycle to take off.

Ava is settled into her room, playing with her toys when I walk toward the back of the house to check on her. "Come on sweet girl; let's get you ready for bed."

"Okay, Momma."

After getting Ava into her nightgown and tucking her into bed, we read a little from her storybook. As I'm reading, she falls asleep, hugging one of her dollies. Mentally tired I kiss her cheek, turn on her night light and turn the lamp off. There's a stack of mail I need to go through and a brand-new bottle of wine I picked up at the store today with my name on it. I change into my sleep shorts and a tank top before heading toward the kitchen. Pouring myself a drink I take it to the couch. The first piece of mail I notice is a large manila envelope, so I open it first. The letterhead is what catches my attention. Vaughn & Vaughn Attorneys at Law. My parents are contesting my legal rights to not only the home I live in, but they are challenging the validity of Grams' Power of Attorney. It states that she wasn't in her right frame of mind due to her illness and that I coerced her into making the decision? *What the hell?*

# 11

## REID

Pulling up in front of Kings Construction, I grab my cut off the seat beside me before sliding out of my truck. It feels so fuckin' good to be back at work. Granted, I'm not at one-hundred percent, so I am unable to work in the field, but coming into the office is a hell of a lot better than sittin' on my ass at home every day. Since Mila and Ava have moved out, I can't take the emptiness of my place anymore. I used to love the peace and solitude I got from living alone, but now everything about my home is off. I miss having Ava's toys scattered around the living room floor. I miss hearing her talk about her day after coming home from preschool. But most of all, I feel lost without Mila. I miss watching her in my kitchen as she would prepare dinner for us. I long for walking into the room and smelling her sweet smell. Now when I'm at home, there are no toys on my floor. There is no soft sound of Ava's laughter. The only thing that remains is Mila's scent. I swear to fuckin' Christ every time I close my eyes at night, I can smell her. That is how much she has imprinted on me. And it takes everything in me not to go and get her and drag her ass back here. Back where she belongs.

Wanting to make sure she is still coming to the party this weekend, I take my phone out of my pocket and send her a quick text.

*Me: Hey Kitten. How's your day so far? How's Ava?*

*Kitten: We're okay. Just dropped Ava at preschool. How are you doing? Are you feeling okay? How was your PT appointment yesterday?*

*Me: PT was good. No more crutches.*

*Kitten: Really!!! That's fantastic!! I'm so proud of you!*

Mila's last reply has me grinning like a fuckin' loon.

*Me: Thanks, babe. Anyway, I wanted to see if you and Ava were still coming to the party this weekend?*

*Kitten: Of course. Ava misses you; she's excited to see you.*

*Me: Is Ava the only one who misses me?*

It takes Mila a minute to reply, and when she does, she gives me the response I was hoping for, and it's officially game fuckin' on.

*Kitten: No. She's not the only one.*

*Me: See you this weekend, gorgeous.*


WALKING in the door of Kings Construction, I'm greeted by our new receptionist Leah. Nikolai hired her a couple of weeks ago. Leah is Alba's friend from school. From what I understand, she was having family issues and was needing a place to stay to get away from said family. With Leyna gone, we needed a new receptionist. She lives with Alba's other friend Sam. I don't know Sam all that well, but he seems like a decent guy, and he's been a good friend to Alba. He even helped the club figure out who was stalking her. Sam is one of the applicants I'm interviewing today. I heard he lost his football scholarship and quit school. Alba said he was working construction before moving with Leah to Polson and was hoping to get hired on at Kings Construction.

"How you doin', sweetheart?" I say to Leah, who is sitting

behind the reception desk. The poor girl looks just as scared and jumpy as she did the first time I saw her at the clubhouse the night she drove Alba home.

Pushing her glasses up her nose, she squeaks out, "Good morning, Mr. Carter."

"You can call me Reid, okay?" After she gives me a shy nod, I rap my knuckles on the counter. "I'll be in the office. When Sam gets here, send him on back."

Thirty minutes later, after grabbing some coffee from the break room and going over today's applicants, I hear a knock on my office door. Looking up from my desk, I see Sam standing at my door waiting for my permission to enter. Tipping my chin and standing I hold my hand out to the kid. "How's it going, man? Come in and have a seat."

Taking my offered hand, Sam answers, "Doing pretty good. I appreciate you taking the time to see me today, Mr. Carter."

This is why I like the kid. Not only did he earn some of my respect when he had the balls to show up at the clubhouse months ago to help Gabriel's woman, he's also respectful. Respect goes a long way with me. "Not a problem, glad you could make it. Your former boss emailed his recommendation, he had nothin' but good things to say about ya. He said he was sorry to see you go," I inform him as we both take our seats.

"Yeah, I liked it there, and I hated leaving my boss short-handed and in a bind, but I did what I had to do for my friend. Her safety is more important."

Once those words leave Sam's mouth, I know I don't need to hear any more. With his glowing recommendation and the fact that he's loyal as fuck to those he cares about, I know this kid is just what we need. "I've heard all I need to kid. I'm giving you the job." Picking up my pen, I scribble an address down on a piece of paper. "Be at this address tomorrow mornin' at 7:00 am sharp."

I follow Sam out of the office and back up to the front. When I round the corner, I see Nikolai standing behind Leah, who's sitting at her desk. He's leaning over the back of her seat with his arms on each side of her and his palms on the desk, caging her in. The poor girl is stiff as a board, and her entire face has turned red as Nikolai mutters something into her ear. A few seconds later, they both realize they have an audience. I look at Sam and see a shit-eating grin on his face, and if possible, Leah's blush turns an even deeper shade of red. Without saying a word to his friend, Sam tips his head to me then leaves.

"How'd the interview go?" Nikolai asks, completely ignoring what just happened.

"I hired him. I have a good feeling about the kid." Deciding to pull a Quinn and be nosey, I ask, "Want to tell me what that was all about?" I motion in Leah's direction as Nikolai follows me back down the hall and into my office. Shrugging his shoulders, "Nothing to tell, yet." Knowing what he means, I let that be the end of the conversation. "Alright, man. I'm going to head out and check on the new job site before calling it a day. Will I be seeing ya at the party this weekend?"

"I wouldn't miss it, man. I'll be there," Nikolai confirms.

---

It's early evening when I make it back home. Usually, I would stop by the clubhouse and have a drink with my brothers, but I'm bone tired. Even though my PT has been cut back to once every two weeks and I'm off the crutches, I'm still not back at one-hundred percent. Not that I'm complaining, because my injuries could have been worse. Hell, I've had worse. I know how lucky I am. Deciding to forgo a shower right now, I head straight to my bedroom, strip off my clothes and sit on the edge of my bed. Reaching down, I take the prosthesis from my leg, then my compression sleeve, and rub the swollen red flesh. Once some of the aches have diminished, I lie back in my bed. Seconds after my head hits my pillow, I'm out.

---

IT'S SATURDAY MORNING, and I'm in my bathroom, staring at my reflection. The dream I woke up from just moments ago has me seeing shit in a whole new light. For the first time in a long time, I feel at peace. The dream started the same as it always does, only this time there was no truck, and there was no death.

"I'm gonna miss you, Reid. I'll even miss the rest of the family. The club-they're my brothers too."

"Fuck, California isn't that far away. I'll be comin' to visit every chance I get."

My brother looks at me, somberly, "I'm not going to California, Reid."

"What the hell you talkin' about, Noah?"

He shakes his head. "It wasn't meant to be. God has a different plan for me. But know that I'm happy, Reid. You don't have to worry about me. You don't have to be sad or angry anymore. Everything is just as it should be. It's time for you to take your life back, Reid."

I'm so confused; all I can do is stare at my brother. After a moment, he speaks again. "Will you do something for me, big brother?"

"I'd do anything for you, Noah. You know that."

"I know Reid. And I know you'll make me proud."

I furrow my brow in confusion. "What do you mean? Noah, you're not making any sense."

"Not right now, I'm not, but soon everything will make sense. And I'm counting on you not to let me down, Reid. I need my big brother to do me one more solid, okay? Promise me."

"I've got your back little brother. I always do," I agree, giving him my word.

He gives me a big smile. "I knew I could count on you."

*My brother's parting words just before I wake up. "Oh, and Reid..."*
*I cut my eyes to him one last time, "Yeah?"*
*"Cut your damn hair."*

So, standing in front of my bathroom mirror with the hair clippers in my hand, I'm going to give Noah what he asked for, I'm cutting my hair. Shaving the sides down to my scalp, I leave a few inches of length on the top. Then I take my razor and finish off the sides. Once I'm done, I look at the person I haven't seen since I lost my brother. I see me. With the sides of my head shaved you can now see my tattoo. The same one Noah had. Only his was on the back of his shoulder. It's a black and grey skull with red roses. Our Pops had the same tat. After he passed Noah and I got the tattoo in his honor. When Noah died, I let my hair grow. Looking in the mirror was a constant reminder that he was no longer here. But now, looking in the mirror, I feel different. I feel him with me. And I'm not only honoring my Pops; I'm also honoring Noah.

Walking back to my room, I dress in a pair of jeans and a black t-shirt and my cut. Grabbing the keys to my bike off my dresser, I make my way to the lift. This will be the first time in a couple of months that I have ridden my bike, and I can't wait to feel the wind on my face. I straddle my bike; then I start it up. I close my eyes and enjoy the rumble and the vibration beneath me. *Fuckin' heaven.*

When I pull up to the clubhouse, I park my bike and make my way around back. As I round the corner, I can already hear talking and laughter. Once I come into view, all talking ceases. Now everyone's eyes are trained on me. All my brothers, including Gabriel, have smiles on their faces, while Bella and Alba both have their mouths hanging open in shock. Neither one of them has ever seen me like this, seen the real me. Quinn is the first to break the silence.

"Long time, no see, motherfucker!"

I walk up to the people I consider family. "Yeah, I know, but better late than never, right?" I catch movement to my right, and I see Prez stepping up to me.

"Glad to see ya, son," he says, pulling me in for a hug.

"Thanks, Prez," I return.

A couple of hours later, I'm sitting outside at a table with my brothers when I feel a set of arms snakes around my neck from behind. Looking over my shoulder, I see Liz, our club whore. Her actions piss me the fuck off. I have no idea what the hell her game is since I haven't touched her ass in over a year. That's when I see Mila standing about ten feet behind us with a look of shock and hurt all over her gorgeous face.

*Son of a bitch.*

With Ava on her hip, she quickly turns around and rushes off in Bella's direction. I don't miss the death glare on Bella's face either. Gripping Liz by her wrists, I toss her arm off me as I stand. Leaning in real close to the bitch's face. "I know what you're trying to do, but your games won't work on me. Don't ever fucking touch me again." I seethe. With a slight shove, Liz teeters back, almost falling. The only thing on my mind right now is Mila.

Striding across the yard, I put myself on a direct path to Mila. I step in front of Bella, who is currently holding Ava while whispering to her friend, warning her of my arrival. "Kitten, I need to speak with you," I demand, taking her hand in mine and leading her across the clubhouse lawn past all the lingering eyes, past Quinn and his obnoxious shit-eating grin and walk inside. Coming to the first door I see, which happens to be a bathroom, I stop. Tugging Mila inside behind me, I close the door and lock it before I press her against it with my body.

"What are you doing?" she asks with a slight pitch to her voice.

"Just wanted to say hi."

She narrows her gold colored eyes at me. "Well, now that you've said it, you can let me go, and go back to your *friend*."

Bringing my face a mere inch from hers, I stress my next words carefully. "Liz is not my friend. She is nothing to me. The whore is just a shit-stirring troll." After a moment, she seems satisfied with my sincerity and nods. With her face a breath away from mine, Mila licks her lips, and states, "You look... different."

Reaching her hand up, she runs her soft, delicate fingers over the tattoo on my freshly shaved head. "I like it," she admits in a low, raspy voice. The words barely leave her mouth when I bring my lips crashing down on hers. We both let out a moan as our tongues make their way into one another's mouth. Both desperately seeking each other's taste. Without thought, I run my palm down the front of Mila's dress and slip my hand underneath until I find what I'm looking for.

"Reid," Mila moans into my mouth as I guide my hand inside of her panties, and I run my finger through her slit, my actions causing her to buck her hips.

"So fuckin' wet for me," I growl. When I see the look in her eyes that says she is starting to overthink things, I lean in and whisper into her ear. "Close your eyes, Kitten, just feel and let me take care of you." As soon as the words leave my mouth, Mila closes her eyes, and her body relaxes entirely into me. Pressing my palm against her clit, I slip one finger inside of her pussy. Feeling how tight she is has me so fuckin' hard, and I wish it were my cock inside of her instead. When I feel her walls begin to tighten around my finger, I rest my forehead against hers. "Come for me, Kitten." As soon as the command leaves my mouth Mila's pussy spasms around my finger, and I take her mouth with mine, swallowing her cry as her orgasm crashes through her.

Once her breathing is back under control, and the fog has lifted from her brain, I feel the change in Mila as she stiffens under me. When I pull back, I can see an embarrassed look on her face, and she refuses to meet my eyes. I'm not having it. "Babe, look at me." When she ignores me and starts to fidget, I tip her chin and force her to look at me. "Don't you dare be embarrassed by what just happened. Watching you come undone was the sexiest thing I've ever seen. And I plan on making you come again, only next time it will be on my cock when I'm deep inside your sweet pussy. When it happens, it damn sure won't be inside a bathroom. It will be at home in my bed, where I will spend all night worshipping your body. Now tell me you get me, Kitten." Mila nods her head, so I ask her again, "I need words, babe."

With a shuttered breath, she gives me what I ask for. "Yeah, Reid. I got you."

Flipping the lock on the bathroom door, I go to take Mila's hand once again only to have her stop me.

"Don't you want to maybe, uh, wash your hand before we go back out there?" she inquires pointing to the hand that she just came all over. Turning my body slightly toward her and looking over my shoulder, I lift the finger that was just inside of her and put it in my mouth, causing Mila's to open hers in shock. Once I've sucked it clean, I give her a wink. "Sweetest thing I ever fuckin' tasted."

# 12

## MILA

I have never gotten off as fast and as hard as I did pressed against the door in that bathroom. I ended up spending the rest of the night riding a high from the fast-paced orgasm Reid gave me. The way he controlled the situation—commanded me. His kiss—His touch provoked so many feelings and caused so many sensations to flood my senses.

When I first noticed him tonight, I was taken aback by his appearance. In a good way. He looked extraordinarily sexy yet so different with his head shaved, exposing that beautiful tattoo. The look suits him. He looked like a new man. He seemed happy.

Lying here in bed hours later, my body is still on fire from our encounter and craving his touch. If he can do what he did in a matter of minutes, what can he do with more time?

---

I FEEL LIGHTER than I've felt in a long time walking to the kitchen to brew some coffee this morning. That is until I notice the contestment papers sitting on the kitchen table, reminding me that nothing is as perfect as it seems to be. Talk about a mood-buster. All I can do is wait until the end of the month to stand in the courtroom in front of the judge to defend my case. For the life of me, I can't understand why they would contest Power of Attorney. I've been the only one to take care of any of Grams' needs since before she was even diagnosed, and I pay what isn't covered by insurance as well. I've never asked anything of them since I left years ago. Sure, she had papers done giving me Power of Attorney after the fact, but she was still of sound mind, enough to understand what she was doing. None of it adds up. Pushing myself off of the table, I start the coffee pot and go about my routine and get Ava up and ready so that I can drop her off at preschool. Walking into her room, I sit down on her bed and rub the top of her nose like I always do to wake her up. She opens her bright blue eyes and smiles up at me. "Morning, sleepyhead. You want cereal or oatmeal for breakfast?" I ask her as she sits up and climbs into my lap.

"Cereal."

I get her dressed and fix her hair into a ponytail before sitting her down to eat and get myself ready for work.

Kate, my former boss, had a job lined up for me after taking care of Reid. Her friend who works at a local nursing home on the other side of town, happened to be looking for someone because they recently had one of their staff leave them. I wasn't sure being in the home care field was right for me. So, she put in some calls, and a couple of days later boom; I was interviewing and getting hired the same day. That and what I made taking care of Reid was starting to run low—too low.

After dropping Ava off, I go to the nursing home Grams resides at. I've made it a point to swing by even if it's only for a few minutes every day to check on her to make sure my parents haven't been causing any problems. Pulling up to the nursing home, I do my best to push all thoughts of my parents in the back of my mind. I run into Joni, her nurse, as I'm walking down the hall. "Hey, Joni." I give her a small wave before stopping."

"Oh, hey, sweetie. How are you doing today?" She greets me.

"I'm good. How's Grams doing today? Any signs of my parents?"

"Today has been a good day." She smiles, saying "And no sign of your parents. I promise if they come around again, I'll be sure to let you know, honey,"

After thanking her, I head to Gram's room and find her sitting in her chair, soaking up the morning sun coming through the window. I set my purse down on her bed and walk in front of her and kneel. "Hey Grams, how are you feeling today?" I ask.

"Mila, my sweet girl. I was just thinking about you. Come, sit, and visit for a minute." She pats the arm of a chair adjacent to hers. I take a seat, and we both sit in silence for a minute while she reaches out and places her hand over mine.

"You look tired, dear. Are you alright?"

"I'm good, Grams."

"You'll tell me in time. You always do. Where's my great-grandbaby?"

"She's at preschool. I brought her for a visit the other day. Do you remember? She drew you that picture hanging on your wall right over there." I point in the direction I'm speaking. She studies the picture for a moment before a tear rolls down her cheek, and it breaks my heart.

"I'm sorry. I don't remember." She lightly squeezes my hand.

"That's okay," I try to comfort her. So far, she gets easily confused, forgets whole days sometimes, or even simple tasks like how to use a fork. Things most people do daily without thinking. And she also gets stuck in the past now and again. All things most everyone takes for granted, I now see in a different light. Every day she smiles and says my name when I walk in the room is more special to me than the next because I know one day I will step in here and she won't know who I am.

I stay and visit another five minutes before heading to work.

When lunchtime rolls around, I get a text from Reid.

*Reid: Hey, babe. How's your day?*

*Me: Good so far.*

*Reid: Wanted you to know I'm thinking about you. I'm thinking about what I want to do to you.*

The last text makes me melt into my seat.

*Me: I'm thinking of you too.*

*Reid: Later, Kitten.*

I DON'T REPLY. The ache between my legs stays with me the rest of the day as I replay his words.

At the end of the day, I pick Ava up, and she asks me on the way home, "Momma, when can we visit Reid?"

"We saw him yesterday, sweetie, at the party."

"But I wanna see him today," she pleads.

"What do you say we pick up a pizza and have a picnic on the living room floor for dinner tonight?" I look in my rear-view mirror and glance at my daughter, who's watching cartoons on my phone. Her head jerks up, and she smiles with excitement, "Weally?! And a movie and ice cweam too?"

I nod my head in approval. "Yep, movie and ice cream too." Hopefully, I can take her mind off Reid for a little while and maybe mine too.

"Yay! Jama party!" She claps her hands, and her giggles fill the air.

I spend the rest of my evening sitting on the floor in the center of a pillow fort, eating junk food while watching a movie with my daughter.

AFTER THE USUAL paperwork in the mornings, I grab my first chart of the day. For now, I have a shift that will allow me to have the evenings and nights off but will need to rotate some weekends and holidays now and then. The hours are a lot better than the shifts I worked at the hospital. I worked wherever and whenever they needed me.

After lunch, I make my way to the nursing station to update my patient's files on the computer when I hear a gruff man's voice call my name. "Mila Vaughn?" I raise my head from looking at the computer screen to see an officer standing in front of me.

"Yes?" I reply. In his outreached hand is a white envelope. "I'm here to serve you papers."

Looking around, I notice a couple of people briefly look at me. Shrugging my shoulders in embarrassment, I ask him, "What for?" I take it from him and tuck the envelope into the shirt pocket of my scrubs.

"I don't know, ma'am. I only deliver them. Have a good day," he says, giving me a sympathetic look before turning to walk away.

My parents come to mind as I finish up my updates and quietly apologize to those around me for the disruption before walking down the hall and stepping outside for some fresh air. Retrieving the envelope out of my pocket, I open it. Notice of Eviction? I thought Grams owned her home? I don't understand any of this, and I need to get to the bottom of it. I don't have much money, but I happen to know a lawyer, and maybe he will be willing to at least give me some advice. The door beside me starts to open, so I stuff the papers back into my pocket and move to the side.

"Mila, I thought I saw you come out here. Is everything okay?" Tracie, my supervisor, asks as she steps outside.

"Everything's okay, Tracie. Just a little unexpected news, but it's nothing I can't handle."

She gives me an understanding nod, "Listen, we need you to stay until 7:00 pm today. I know you have a daughter in preschool, so I wanted to give you a heads up."

I guess I can call Bella to pick Ava up for me and see if she would keep her until I get off work. I hate to ask her, but she is the only person besides myself on the approved pick up list at Ava's preschool. "I'm going to call someone who can pick up my daughter," I tell Tracie.

"Sure. Come find me when you get finished," she says and walks back inside. Digging my phone out of my pocket, I bring up Bella's number and dial.

"Hey, girl. What up?" she answers.

"Hey. I need a big favor."

"Sure," she says

I let out a heavy sigh, "Could you pick up Ava for me? They need me to work a few hours over my normal time today."

"I can do that. I was going to visit Alba after work, so Ava can play with Gabe," Bella happily tells me.

I hate asking and burdening people, but sometimes I don't have a choice. "Thank you. Listen, I need to get back to work. I'll let you know when I'm on my way. Do I need to pick her up at your place or Alba's?

"I'll probably be at Alba's since the guys have something going on out at the clubhouse this evening," she tells me.

"Okay. Thanks again, Bella."

"You're welcome. We'll see you later," she says before we hang up, and I head back into the building.

By the time I leave work, I'm dragging and ready to pick up Ava and head home. It's not a long drive to Alba's home from work, so it doesn't take me long to pull into her driveway. I don't even reach the door before it opens, and a pregnant Alba greets me. I think Gabriel's goal is to keep that woman pregnant. "Hey, Alba," I welcome her.

"Come in, we already had something to eat, and I just finished giving the kids baths and putting Gabe down."

"You're the best. Thank you. As tired as I am, I was going to get fast food and put us straight to bed tonight," I say, following her into the kitchen.

"While Bella is upstairs putting some clean clothes on Ava, I'm going to grab you a plate of food. We had plenty of lasagna leftover from dinner. You can eat before you go."

I take a seat at her kitchen island as she sets a plate of warm food in front of me. It smells so good. I put the first bite in my mouth and savor the flavors. I'm always so busy that I don't get a lot of home-cooked meals like this. The kind that tastes like they've been simmering all day.

Alba laughs. "You hungry?"

"Starving," I tell her, taking another bite.

"Momma!" My little girl bounds into the kitchen, still full of energy. Scooping her up, I place her on my knee and continue to eat. "Did you have fun today?" I engage her. Her little eyes light up with enthusiasm.

"I want a baby brother, Momma," she says with certainty, causing me to swallow my food the wrong way and cough. "A brother?" I spit out as Alba hands me a glass of water with an amused look on her face.

"Yep, I want a baby like Gabe. Aunt Alba has a baby in her tummy. Can you put a baby in your tummy for me too, Momma?"

Bella and Alba stand there looking on waiting to see how I handle the situation. I don't even know how to handle the situation, so I ignore it altogether and kiss the top of her head instead. "Thanks so much for watching her tonight," I tell them as I scrape my partially eaten dinner in the trash and place the plate in the sink.

"Anytime," Bella replies.

"You ready to go home, sweetie?" I ask a very sleepy looking Ava.

They both walk us out, and we say our goodbyes before I load up and head home. Even my little girl seems to have had a long day because she fell asleep a couple of minutes ago. As I'm making the turn toward my neighborhood, I notice a lot of traffic and up ahead a couple of police cars and fire trucks with their lights flashing. *I hope everything is okay.* After I get closer, I can see the officers standing outside their cars talking to people and several residents turning around. Rolling up to what looks like a checkpoint, I roll my car window down. "Hi, Officer. What's going on?" I inquire as I observe the frustrated faces of a few of my neighbors as they drive by in their cars.

"There's a gas leak, and we have to evacuate several blocks for everyone's safety. Do you live here?"

"Yes, over on Crowne Circle. Please don't tell me that I can't go home." I slump back in my seat.

"I'm afraid I can't let any residents in until the gas company has fixed the issue, and the area is deemed safe to re-enter."

Perfect, this was just what I needed after today. "How will we know when we can return home?" I ask him.

"The gas company usually will inform you by a phone call that it's safe to return."

I turn and look back at Ava, who is still sleeping in her car seat and think about what I do now. I don't want to burden anyone or put them out with me suddenly needing a place to stay, so I opt to spend the money and find a hotel room for the night. I thank the officer for his patience and turn my car around and head toward town. I decide on a hotel about two blocks from the downtown main street, although my money situation mostly chooses it for me because it happens to be the cheapest. With Ava in my arms, I walk in and make way to the check-in counter pay for a room and receive my key card for room 68. At least it's floor level and I don't have to climb the stairs. As soon as the door clicks open after I insert the card Ava pops her eyes open, raises her head and looks around while rubbing her sleepy eyes. "What's dis place, Momma?"

"This is where we get to sleep tonight, sweetie."

"Why?" she asks as I inspect the bed before laying her down on it.

"It's okay, baby. Go back to sleep," I tell her. There's no need for me to explain a gas leak to a sleepy four-year-old. Closing her eyes, she curls up to hold her dolly, and I tuck the covers around her. Needing to unwind a little, I turn on the TV, hoping to find something to take my tired mind off everything.

I don't know when it happened, but after I kicked off my shoes and propped myself up next to Ava on the bed, I fell asleep. Banging on the hotel door startles me. Whoever it is, they are being persistent and have started jiggling the door handle. I walk over to the curtains and carefully peek through the window to see who it is. A large guy wearing all black is standing outside the door. He spots me looking at him, then steps back and starts kicking in the door. Complete panic sets in. I run and grab Ava, who has already woken at this point and looks scared to death. I take her to the bathroom and sit her in the tub while she starts to cry. "Momma," she says through terrified sobs.

"Sweetie, listen to me," Looking back over my shoulder as the pounding continues, I say, "You stay here. Momma has to call a policeman. No matter what, you leave the door locked. Don't open for anyone. Do you understand?" I rush out in urgency, knowing any moment the door is going to give. She clings to her dolly with tear-filled eyes as I close the shower curtain, lock the bathroom door and close it behind me. Once I know my daughter is safe, I dart over to the phone on the nightstand to dial 911. As soon as I have the receiver in my hand, the door bursts open and a guy wearing a face mask charges me. My reaction time isn't quick enough. The only place I have to go is over the bed. The stranger grabs me, slapping my face hard enough that I taste blood, then he throws my body across the room. I hit my head on the corner of the dresser, causing my vision to blur, and I lose my footing and stumble to the floor. While I'm down, his booted foot hits my side with so much force the wind gets knocked out of me. Coughing from the pain, I suck air in trying to catch my breath as he yanks me by my hair, pulling me to my feet. I struggle trying to break free from his hold, but he quickly overpowers me and rears back, punching me in the face then tosses me atop the bed. Still dazed from the blow, I roll over to try and reach the base of the phone, still sitting on the table beside the bed as blood drips from my nose. I have it in my grasp as he pulls me, rolling my body over. Using the momentum, I knock him upside his head with it. He climbs on the bed and straddles me. Hovering over the top of my body, looking down at me unfazed by the blow, he backhands me one more time. His dark, cold eyes are the only physical feature I can see behind the mask he's wearing. His large hands suddenly wrap around my neck, slowly applying pressure. I punch, kick, and scratch at his arms with everything I've got to free myself, but he only tightens the stranglehold he has on my throat, constricting my airway further. My vision starts to cloud around the edges as I fight to breathe—fight for my life.

# 13

## REID

I'm sitting behind my desk at work, thinking about Mila. I can't get the image of her beautiful face as she came out of my head. I also decided to give her a few days to come to terms with what happened between us and what is going to happen between us very soon. It's taking everything I have for me to not go over to her house, throw her over my shoulder and take her home with me where she belongs. But I can't risk scaring her off, not that I'd let her run. Mila is mine. Her fate was sealed the first day she showed up at my place banging on my door and throwing her sass around as she looked at me with those hypnotizing eyes of hers.

I'm pulled from my thoughts when I feel my phone vibrate in my pocket. Taking it out, I see a text from Quinn.

**Dipshit:** *Get your ass off that damn computer and come to the clubhouse for a drink with me.*

**Me:** *Fuck off, how do you know I'm working?*

**Dipshit:** *I'm outside, asshole. Now let's go.*

**Me:** *Give me five.*

.  .  .

SHAKING MY HEAD, I turn off my computer before standing up and grabbing my cut off the back of my chair and sliding it on. After I flick all the lights in the office off and set the alarm, I make my way outside to see Quinn sitting on his bike, smoking a cigarette. Without a word, I lift my chin toward my brother as I straddle my bike. As we ride down the street and breathe in the warm summer air, something out of the corner of my eye catches my attention. Letting off the throttle, I begin to slow down. Parked at a piece of shit motel is Mila's car.

*What the fuck. Why would she be at a motel?*

When I turn into the motel parking lot, I know my brother is right behind me, and when I glance in his direction, I see he's also noticed Mila's car and is also wondering the same shit as me.

Quinn and I both dismount our bikes at the same time and make our way to the check-in office. When we walk in the bell on the door, alerts the old lady behind the desk to our arrival.

"Need a room?" she asks.

"No, ma'am. I want to know what room Mila Vaughn is staying in." After I repeat myself to the old bat two times because she can't hear shit, she is reluctant to give up the information until she eyes mine and Quinn's cut.

"She's in room 68. I don't want no trouble, ya hear me, young man?"

"I'm not looking for trouble, lady." After eyeing me wearily for a moment, the old lady hands me the key card to Mila's room. Taking it from her wrinkled hand, I nod my head in thanks before turning on my heel and walking out.

Walking along the side of the building, Quinn and I head in the direction of room 68. As we approach the door, my senses go on high alert, and my heart rate picks up. I immediately reach into my cut and draw my piece. I don't have to look to know my brother has made the same observation as me and has done the same. Because Mila's motel door is open and on closer inspection, it has been busted down. With Quinn at my back, I place the palm of my hand against the door and slowly open it. What I see in front of me has my stomach knotting, and my vision is seeing red. Some motherfucker is straddling Mila, and he has his hands wrapped around her throat. I notice her leg gives one final jolt of fight before her whole body goes limp. Suddenly, I charge the motherfucker and tackle him to the floor beside the bed. I repeatedly land blow after blow after blow to his face. I don't know how much time had passed or when the guy underneath me stopped moving; Quinn grabbing my shoulder is what snaps me out of my frenzied state.

"Don't kill him yet, brother. Not if you want some answers."

Quinn's right. I want to know why the fuck Mila is staying in this room in the first place, and why this piece of shit tried to kill her. With my thoughts snapping back to Mila, I turn my attention away from the bloody man lying on the floor to my woman. Seeing her beaten and passed out body on the bed has my fingers itchin' to put a bullet in the motherfucker's head.

"I already checked her pulse, and she's still breathin'. You want to take her to the hospital, or do you want me to call Doc?" Quinn asks.

"No hospital right now. Hospital means cops and no way are the cops gettin' their hands on him," I say, gesturing toward the man still passed out. "He's mine," I declare.

"You got it, brother."

With Quinn on the phone, I begin to take in Mila's injuries. A split lip, a busted eye, and the purple and blue finger marks around her neck from where the guy tried to take life away from her. A moan escaped her mouth, and her one good eye flutters open. "Kitten, can you hear me? You're going to be alright. I've got you," I assure her as I stroke her hair. Opening her mouth, Mila struggles to say something, and in a rough, scratchy voice, she's able to get one word out.

"Ava?"

My stomach drops. How in the hell could I forget about Ava? Quinn suddenly pipes up, "She's in the bathroom, brother, but I can't get her to open the door. All I hear is her crying."

Rushing over to the bathroom door, I drop down to my knees and begin to talk gently. "Ava, sweetheart, can you unlock the door for me." The sounds of her sobs breaking my heart before I hear her sweet voice.

"Reid?"

"Yeah, baby girl, it's me. Can you come out for me?" A second later, I hear the lock click over, and a crying, shaking Ava throws her tiny body into my waiting arms. She buries her face into my neck as I rub her back and try calming her down. I step back into the bathroom, so I can shield her from the view of what's in the room. I do not want the vision of her battered mother and a bloody, beaten man ingrained into her memory. No child should have to witness such a thing.

"Doc, Gabriel, and Prez are on their way," Quinn informs me. "Want me to take Ava so you can go to your woman?"

Coaxing Ava to release a little bit of her hold on me, I ask, "You think you can go see Quinn a minute for me, sweetheart? I promise I'm not going anywhere." Looking at me with her big blue eyes, she blinks away a few more tears before she looks over at Quinn and then nods her head. "Good girl." I praise her by kissing her on top of her head before passing her off to my brother. The same time I'm walking back over to where Mila lays, Prez, followed by Doc and Gabriel burst into the motel room with murder in their eyes as they take in the scene. Doc doesn't waste any time tending to Mila while Gabriel handles the soon-to-be-dead man on the floor. I turn my attention back to Doc when he begins to speak.

"Let's get her back to the clubhouse so that I can do a more thorough exam. She's pretty busted up. No signs of sexual assault.

Nothing we can't handle. Unless you want to take her to the hospital? It's your call."

I'm about to open my mouth when Mila rouses. "Where's Ava? Reid, where is she?"

Leaning over the bed, I scoop Mila into my arms. "Shh baby, she's alright, Quinn has her. We're gonna get you out of here, okay?"

"Okay, but no hospital, and I don't want Ava to see me like this," Mila pleads.

"Alright, Kitten, let's go."

When I make it outside with Mila in my arms, I notice Logan and Bella have shown up. Once I climb into the van with Jake, I look out the window and see Quinn walking out of the motel room with Ava, and he strides straight toward Bella, who quickly takes her from him. Satisfied that Ava is taken care of, I give Jake the go-ahead for us to leave.

An hour later, we are back at the clubhouse. Mila has been checked out by Doc, and I have cleaned her up the best I can. She woke up and was alert not long after we arrived, and she was able to tell us what she remembered. She said her neighborhood had a gas leak, and the police department wasn't letting anyone in, so instead of calling me, she decided to stay at a motel. To say I was pissed was an understatement. I don't understand why the hell she didn't call me. She insisted it was late, and she didn't want to burden anyone. How could she be so stupid to think her or Ava would ever be a burden? I told her as much too. Her sassy ass had to pipe up and tell me she could take care of herself. And my response was simple. "I get that you've been on your own and have had to take care of yourself and Ava, but no more, Kitten. You two have me now, you have the club." By the time I was finished speaking my peace, Mila was crying. I held her until she stopped and fell asleep. Once I knew she was out and would be for awhile since Doc gave her some medicine for her pain, I slipped out of my room and headed in the direction of the basement on a mission. The mission involved the motherfucker who thought he could put his filthy hands on my woman and live to see another day.

Walking into the basement, I'm met with Prez, Gabriel, and Quinn. Tied to a metal chair in the middle of the room is a man who is about to draw his last breath. The detached look on his face tells me he knows his time has come, and this is the end of the road for him.

Not wanting to waste any more time on this cocksucker than necessary because I have better things to do, like getting back to my woman, I walk directly in front of the man who is taking up more time than he deserves. "I want to know what the fuck your plans were tonight and why."

"Got paid five grand to take the bitch out."

As soon as the word bitch leaves his mouth, my fist lands a solid punch to his jaw. "Watch it, motherfucker. What you say will determine how fast or how slow I take your worthless life tonight." The shadow that crosses the guy's bloody face lets me know he understands what my words mean. He gives us what we want, and his death will be quick; he fights us, and he'll be wishing he was never born.

"I don't know the details. I met a guy a few days ago, a couple of towns over, at a gas station. He paid me five grand cash and gave me the girl's address and her description. I asked him how he wanted the job done." He shrugs his shoulders. "Some clients like the target to be taken out quickly, some painfully. I charge accordingly. I told him the job would be two grand. He told me he'd give me an extra three if I took care of the kid too. The suit said he didn't care, just that it needed to be done ASAP. I followed the chick for two days. I was going to take her out in her house, but she and the kid ended up at the hotel." The mention of Ava causes a deep growl to rise from deep within, and I take a step further in the man's direction before he is quick to interject.

"Wait a minute. I don't touch fuckin' kids, man. I took the suit's money, but no way was I killing a kid," the dirty prick confesses.

"Does the suit have a name?" I question with clenched fists.

"No, I never exchange names with clients. All I can tell you is the man was around six-foot-one, black hair and maybe mid-forties. The guy had money written all over him."

From the pictures I found online when researching her parents, along with the fact that they showed up in town, I'm almost positive who is behind this shit. I can't believe the heartless bastards are even going after Ava, their own granddaughter. But my question is, *why*? I may not know the answers, but I'm sure as hell going to find out. I've gotten all I need to know from this motherfucker. Looking the guy dead in his eyes, I reach into my cut and wrap my hand around the cold metal of my gun before taking it out. Resolved in my choice, I aim it directly between the eyes of the man sitting in front of me and pull the trigger.

## 14

## MILA

"Where's Ava?" As every muscle in my body screams in protest with the movement, I push up, trying to prop myself on the pillow. I don't know how long I've been asleep, but it feels like forever.

"Bella has her, babe. She's in the room across the hall fast asleep," Reid comforts me, taking my hand in his.

I can't help but replay the attack over and over again. I want to say I'm okay, but the truth is—I'm scared out of my mind.

"You want me to go get her, beautiful?"

"No. Not until I have a chance to clean myself up. I don't want her to see me like this. Nothing about me is beautiful right now," I tell him. I don't want to think about how frightened she was sitting in that bathroom, listening, and not knowing what was happening. I look at Reid. "I would like to take a shower."

"I'll go get one started," he says, standing, then leans down and kisses my forehead. I close my eyes and focus on the gentle touch of his lips against my skin, trying to calm my racked nerves. After he disappears into the bathroom, I take a moment to look at my surroundings. Being here—not just in the clubhouse, but in his room amongst his things in his bed, I feel safe. What made that man choose me as his victim? Was it because I was alone with a child? I wouldn't think he wanted to rob me because he was so intent on hurting—no, he wanted to kill me. Reid walks out of the bathroom toward me. He pulls back the covers and tosses them to the side, then bends down and scoops me into his strong arms. Part of me wants to protest. A much more significant part of me finds too much comfort in the warmth of his embrace. Carrying me into the bathroom, Reid gently helps me stand. I hiss at the pain in my side with the slight movement. I can almost guarantee I have at least bruised ribs.

"Shit, babe, I'm sorry," Reid looks on with worry.

"I'm okay. Once I can stand under the flow of that hot water, it's sure to soothe some of the soreness." Before I can reach for the hem of my scrubs, Reid grabs my hand, stopping me. Without a word, he takes the hem and starts to pull upwards. Slowly raising my arms above my head, I let him gently pull my top off. Stepping behind me, he unclasped my bra and slides the straps over my shoulders, exposing my breasts before dropping it to the floor beside my shirt. My breath hitches. The whole scene is a reenactment of the way I took care of him weeks ago. My heart starts to pound harder in my chest. As he moves to stand directly in front of me, I hold my breath and wait to see what he'll do next. His eyes never leave mine as his hands glide with ease down the curve of my waist and rest briefly on my hips before hooking his thumbs into the waistband of my pants, peeling them from my body. Grabbing hold of his broad shoulders, I lift my feet to step out of them. Now completely exposed to him, Reid continues with his eye contact as he stands. Without hesitation, I watch him strip from his clothes as well. I feel my core temperature rise at the sight of his body. Taking in every detail.

He takes me by the hand, and he guides me into the walk-in shower, closing the glass door as he steps inside, not giving a second thought to getting his prosthesis wet. The moment the hot water cascades over my body my tension lessens, my muscles start to relax, and I close my eyes. Just after I turn around, so the water is hitting my front, I hear the snap of a shampoo bottle. His hands tangle in my hair as his fingers gently massage the citrus-scented shampoo into my scalp, causing me to moan. He reaches up grabbing the detachable shower head and starts to rinse my hair. I spin back around to face him. Squeezing some body wash into the palm of his hand, he steps closer and lightly splays his hands over my chest. His touch teasing as he drags them down my sides, grazing the sides of my breasts along the way before sweeping across my stomach. He brings them up between my breasts only to repeat the same path all over again. Kneeling, he starts at my feet washing his way up my leg, stopping mere inches from the one place I want him most. My lips part when he looks at me with want. Continuing, he repeats the same process with the other leg, pausing inches from my aching pussy. Without warning, his tongue darts out tasting me. I throw my head back as his mouth works magic on my clit. Reaching down, I run my fingers over his scalp as he devours me. My legs soon begin to quiver with my building orgasm causing my hands to grip his hair tighter. Reaching behind me, he grabs a handful of my ass pulling my hips forward just as my orgasm explodes. My release is so strong, I almost blackout.

Suddenly overcome with so much emotion, I begin to cry. Carefully rising, Reid rinses the suds from my body then turns off the water. Taking my face in the palm of his hands, he kisses me. It's not like the kiss that day at the party. It's softer—sweeter. Coming to my senses, knowing I should return the favor, I reach down and run the length of his cock with the tips of my fingers.

"Kitten, this isn't about me, it's about you." He groans when I touch him again.

Gently stopping me, he states, "Soon, beautiful. You need to heal first."

At that moment, the words 'I love you' were at the forefront of my mind and almost on the tip of my tongue. After he towel-dries me, Reid helps me dress in a pair of his sweatpants and one of his shirts.

"I know they're huge, but they're all I've got," he expresses.

"That's okay. It's perfect," I tell him. They smell like him, and I find it comforting.

"Come on, let's get you settled in bed," he tells me.

Stopping in front of the mirror, I look at myself. Busted lip, black eye and purple marks covering my neck. My daughter is safe, and I'm alive. Right now, that's all that matters. Climbing into bed, I realize I need Ava with me. "Could you bring Ava in here? I know it's late, and she's asleep, but I need to hold her for awhile," I tell him.

"Sure," he says with understanding. Once he finishes getting dressed, he walks out of the room and reappears with Ava, and I snuggle her close to my chest. I came so close to never seeing her sweet face again. So close to never hearing her say *Momma* or *I love you* again. Holding back tears, I look up at Reid. "Thank you," I whisper.

"I'll be in the room next door if you need me," he responds, heading toward the bedroom door.

"Stay," I say, causing him to pause with his hand on the doorknob. "Please," I beg.

Shifting his weight, he turns and strides toward the other side of the bed, takes care of removing his prosthesis, and climbs in behind me. He kisses my neck before placing his hand on my hip. It doesn't take me long before the sweet sounds of my daughter's breathing cause my eyes to get heavy with sleep, and they begin to close.

I WAKE to a soft little finger stroking my nose. I open my eyes to see Ava staring at me.

"You got a boo-boo, Momma." Her tiny hand touches my eye.

"I know, sweetie."

"Bad man hurt you?" she asks

Before I can respond, I hear Reid clear his throat and look up to see him standing at the foot of the bed with a plate in his hand and a coffee mug in the other. "Ava and I made you breakfast. She fixed you some toast with strawberry jam." He smiles. An excited Ava jumps off the bed and retrieves the plate from him and carefully carries it, gently placing it next to me on the bed.

"I put da strawberry jams on by myself," she giggles as she eagerly waits for me to take a bite.

"It's delicious. Thank you, sweetie," I express, causing her face to light up with happiness. Reid hands me my coffee, and I sip on it while Ava steals a bite of my breakfast.

"Bella is here. Would it be okay if she took Ava for a little while today? We need to talk," he says.

I'm not sure what we would need to talk about other than what happened last night. "I don't mind."

"She's downstairs, and she brought you some clothes. I'll send her up."

I don't know how well that's going to work. Bella is much shorter than I am. Leaning down, he kisses me then leaves. Ava climbs onto the bed and sits cross-legged, and starts brushing her doll's hair. There is a light knock on the bedroom door, followed by Bella entering the room and closing the door behind her. Holding up a bag, she greets me. "I have some clothes, and before you say it, I raided Alba's closet for them. You two are close in height and size. At least she kept it basic. Jeans, black t-shirt, and a pair of sandals."

"Thanks," I tell her.

Getting out of bed, I strip out of Reid's clothes and start to put on the others. Surprisingly, my ribs are feeling much better. I look down at the bruises covering my side before slipping the shirt over my head.

I walk into the bathroom to do something with my hair. Bella leans against the door frame and looks over her shoulder before asking, "You doing okay?"

"Besides being sore, I'm fine. If you're asking emotionally, that's hard to say right now. My feelings are a bit all over the place. I'm grateful the guys found me when they did. I'm scared; I'm confused. Inside, I'm a mess," I admit to her.

"I understand. Just know I'm here if you need to talk, and Reid will take care of you and Ava. As far as the attacker, I don't know what became of him. I didn't ask, and the guys wouldn't tell."

The three of us make our way downstairs to the sounds of men talking. We find Reid, Quinn, and Jake sitting at the bar.

"I'm going to take off. I told Alba I'd meet her at the park by the library in about an hour. Ava, give your momma hugs so we can go play," she announces.

I hug and kiss my baby girl goodbye. No sooner do they walk out the door when Reid is at my side. "Come on. Let's go sit in the kitchen."

I follow him into the kitchen and sit down in the chair he offers. "Listen, I've got something to tell ya." He faces his chair toward me and sits. "The guy who attacked you was a hitman. I suspect from his confession and description of the person who paid him to do it, that it may have been your father." He looks at me with certainty. *But why? My parents?*

"I don't understand. Why would my parents want me dead? I mean nothing to them. It doesn't make any sense. You must be mistaken," I tell him, feeling a little-light head with his admission.

"I'll get to the bottom of this, I promise, Mila. Is there anything you can tell me—anything at all that might help me figure this all out?"

My brain is overloaded right now, trying to process what I just heard. Do they hate me so much they wish I were dead? But still... Why? I think about the house and eviction papers. But again, I can't make sense of it all. Grams' house isn't worth a whole lot. What would they get out of it? "A few days ago, I received some papers in the mail from my parents' firm in New York. They've filed a motion to contest my Power of Attorney rights with Grams—"

Reid interrupts my confession, "Why didn't you say anything?"

"Let me finish. Yesterday while I was at work, an officer showed up serving me papers. My parents had me served an eviction notice. They are trying to kick me out of our home. How can they even do that?" I bury my face in my hands. Leading me from my seat, Reid guides me to sit on his lap and places his hand between my knees.

"I swear, I'll figure this all out, Kitten," he comforts me.

*Can he?* I still have to fight everything. I still need to stand in a courtroom with the two of them. How am I going to be able to go head-to-head with two prominent attorneys? "Did you guys grab my stuff from the motel room last night? I need my phone. I'm going to give River a call and see if he can help explain what my options are with all the legal stuff my parents are throwing at me," I explain to Reid.

"Who the fuck is River?" he asks defensively.

"The guy I walked out with at Ava's preschool a few weeks ago. He happens to be a lawyer. I figured since we're friends, he might be able to at least give me some free advice on how to handle the situation," I state.

"If I wasn't clear enough last night, Kitten, from now on, it's **us**. All the way, so **we** will be going to see him **together**."

## 15

## REID

What the fuck kind of name is River? A chick name, that's what it is. Mila's giggling has me cutting my eyes over to her, where she is sitting in the passenger seat of my truck. Even with a bruised face, she is the most gorgeous woman I have ever seen. "What's so funny?"

"I can hear you grumbling from over here. And River is a perfectly fine name," she scolds. "I already told you earlier you didn't have to come with me. River is just a friend and a nice guy."

"Nice guy my ass, I saw the way he was lookin' at you the day we picked Ava up from preschool. The motherfucker wants in your pants, and that shit is not happening."

"Just because a guy is nice to a woman doesn't mean he wants to 'get in her pants.' I want you to be kind to him when we get there Reid, I mean it."

"Kitten, he's a man, and you're a beautiful woman, so yes, he most certainly wants to get into your pants. I'll be nice as long as he knows his place is a professional one and that your pussy belongs to me." I watch as Mila's face turns red. She's probably thinking about what happened in the shower. One taste of her

CRYSTAL DANIELS & SANDY ALVAREZ

sweet pussy, and I'm hooked. Fuck, just thinking about it has my dick hard as a fuckin' rock right now. Reaching down I adjust myself, and I don't miss the way Mila has spotted my current state. Glancing back at her, I give her a grin letting her know I'm thinkin' about it too. When she licks her lips, I almost have it in mind to turn this truck around and take her home for another taste.

"Unless you want me showin' up to the lawyer's office with a hard-on, you better quit lookin' at me like that, Kitten." At my warning, Mila snaps her eyes away from my crotch to my face, and I watch her pupils dilate. She is just as affected by me as I am by her. My parking and turning the truck off is what has her breaking out of her daze. "Stay there; I'll come around to get ya," I command as I hop out of my truck. Once I help Mila out of the truck, I wrap my arm around her and pull in close to me as we make our way inside the building where River's office is.

"May I help you?" A young woman sitting behind the reception desk asks us, and I don't miss the double-take she gives Mila. Not surprising considering her bruised face. "I'm Mila Vaughn; I'm here to see River. I don't have an appointment, but could you check to see if he will see me?" Mila asks.

"Sure, you two have a seat over there," she points to her left, where there are a few chairs lined against the wall, "and I'll let Mr. Knight know you're here."

Our asses barely hit our seats before River strides in our direction from down the hall. His steps falter as Mila and I both stand to greet him. "Holy shit, Mila. Are you okay? What happened?" he rushes out. When River's eyes cut to me, and he stands a little taller, I know what the fucker is thinking. "I suggest you wipe that fuckin' look off your face. I'd never put my hands on any woman, especially not **MY** woman/" I square off. Mila, sensing the severity of my tone, places her hand on my arm and gives a light squeeze as she looks directly at the man in front of us.

"River, I was attacked last night. Reid is the one who saved me. He would never hurt me," she tells him with conviction.

"I'm sorry. I apologize for assuming. I was stunned by your appearance, but that's still no excuse." After a few tense moments, I nod my head and accept his apology.

"So, what can I do for you today?" River asks as he sits down behind his desk. Mila and I take our seats across from him. To my left, Mila reaches into her purse, pulls out both envelopes, and hands them to River. "I received the first set of papers in the mail; then, I was served the eviction notice while at work." We both watch on as the lawyer reads over the document. "Susan Vaughn is contesting your rights as Power of Attorney over your grandmother and trying to evict you from your home," he states.

"Yes, and I want to know what I need to do for them not to have control over Grams' care. My parents have not spoken or seen Grams or me in years. Now suddenly, they show up demanding to take over. I can't let that happen, River. I need help," Mila pleads, and I hate how desperate her voice sounds. "I have no idea what they could want. The only thing of value my grandmother has is our house, but I don't see my parents putting up a fight for an old house."

Cutting in, I ask, "Mila mentioned you're her grandmother's attorney. Does she have a will? Do you have any information that could help us to understand what her parents are after?"

"Yes, I am her attorney, and yes, your grandmother has a will, but I'm sorry it would be against the law for me to disclose what is in it with you."

Slumping in her seat, Mila looks defeated. "I understand. Would you at least be willing to take on my case? I don't know how much you charge for services, and I don't have much money, but maybe you would be willing to work out a payment plan with me?"

Cutting in again, I offer, "I'll pay for whatever you need, babe.

Don't worry." When I see her mouth open about to protest, I shake my head and give her a sharp look. "What did we talk about earlier, Kitten?" Remembering our earlier conversation, Mila's face softens before blowing out a deep breath and nods her head in agreement. I know it's tough for her to accept help. When you're used to doing things on your own for so long, you are wary of leaning on another person. It makes me so fuckin' happy she has enough trust in me to allow herself to give in to my help. She and Ava belong to me now, and I am going to prove my worth. Each day we spent together, she was opening up to me more and more. Mila has yet to give any details about Ava's father. I know I could use my hacking skills to try and dig up the information, but I can't bring myself to do it. I already dug into her parents' background and what their end game is with their daughter, but tapping into something like Ava's father and going behind Mila's back on something so personal doesn't sit well with me. I'm willing to be patient and let her come to me when she is ready.

We have just said our goodbyes to River, and he has agreed to take on Mila's case and are about to leave when she excuses herself to the restroom. I'm walking out of River's office when he stops me. "If your reputation precedes you, I trust you'll find the answers you are looking for. I'm sorry I couldn't be of more help, but I'm confident you don't need it."

Well, fuck me. River just permitted me to dig around in his system. Not that I needed it.

"How are ya feelin', babe?" I ask Mila once we make it home. I opted to come back to my place instead of the clubhouse. After we left the lawyer's office, Mila received a text from Alba asking if Ava could stay the night with her and Gabriel. It appears she has taken a shine to baby Gabe. Ava is utterly obsessed with my brother's little boy.

I've never given too much thought to having a family of my

own, but now that I have Mila and Ava, I sure as fuck see it now. I like the idea of Mila giving me a son.

"I feel good. A little tired, but my ribs aren't too sore anymore, and my head has stopped hurting. Whatever Doc gave me last night seems to have done the trick," she says with a yawn. I lead her down the hall. "Come on and take a nap."

She doesn't protest when I lead her past the room she and Ava shared when they were staying here and into my room. Opening my dresser drawer, I take out a t-shirt and hand it to her. Mila accepts my offering, then makes her way to the bathroom to change. While she readies herself, I stride back into the kitchen for a bottle of water and some pain reliever. When I step back into the bedroom, Mila has already crawled into bed. Sitting down on the edge of the bed, I hand over the medicine and twist the cap off the water before passing it to her. Without a word, she takes medicine and downs half the water. Leaning over, I kiss her lips softly. "Sleep, Kitten."

Several hours later, night has fallen, and I'm sitting in the chair beside my bed and watching as Mila begins to stir. "Hey," she rasps in a sleepy voice. "How long was I out?"

"About four hours."

"Really? And have you been watching me the whole time?"

Without lying, I answer, "Yes." I watch as Mila's breathing picks up as we continue to stare at each other. Sitting up in bed, she slowly lifts the blanket away from her body, exposing the curve of her hips and her long, toned legs as she swings them over the edge of the bed and stands. My eyes hone in on the sway of her hips as she moves across the room toward me with purpose. When she steps between my spread legs, I lean forward and place my hands on either side of her legs at her knees. I start to slowly run my hands up the backside of her thighs to the soft curve of her ass. I don't miss the way her skin prickles from my touch.

Mila grips the bottom of the t-shirt she is wearing and pulls it off over her head. Her action is letting me know she's made her choice. I'd be a crazy fucking bastard not to take what she is offering. Standing in front of me in nothing but a black lace thong is the most stunning creature God has ever created. Every inch of this woman is perfect. I take my time studying her magnificent body, from the flare of her hips, all the way up to her full breasts. With my hands still on her, I hook my thumbs into the sides of her panties and slide them down her legs. Once I have them off, I grab hold of her ass, urging her forward. With Mila's sweet-smelling pussy right in front of my face, I lean forward and swipe my tongue through her wet slit. She places her hands on my head and tips her head back letting a groan escape her mouth. I'll never get enough of her taste. Reclining back in the chair, Mila follows by straddling my hips. When she settles onto my lap, I can feel the heat of her pussy through my jeans. In this new position, I cup her breast and swirl my tongue around one of her pink nipples before taking it into my mouth.

"Reid," Mila rasps while digging her nails into my scalp.

My name on her lips is my undoing. With one arm under her ass and the other wrapped around her back, I stand, and she wraps her legs around my waist as I waste no time striding toward the bed. Without a word, she slides out of my arms and bends down to her knees on the floor in front of me. Reaching up, she unbuckles my belt and then my jeans before pulling them down my hips, taking my boxers with them and causing my cock to spring free. Mila places her hands on my stomach, urging me to sit back on the bed. Once I comply, she guides my jeans the rest of the way, exposing my prosthesis. Surprisingly, I have no anxiety at her seeing me. I trusted her once already before giving her that part of me. She has shown nothing but acceptance. This is who I am. With Mila, I don't feel embarrassed. I finally feel comfortable in my own skin. She makes me confident in this part of me. So when she takes it upon herself to remove it, I don't object.

Looking at me, Mila begins to pepper kisses up my scared leg and up the inside of my thigh until she reaches my hard cock. Taking it in her hand, she takes the swollen head of my dick into her warm mouth. "Goddamn it! That feels so fuckin' good, Kitten," I hiss. My words encourage her as she takes me further into her mouth. After a few minutes, I fist my hand around her long, silky hair and lightly tug her off my cock. "Come here," I demand. "When I come, I want it to be inside of you."

Snagging her around the waist, I swiftly twist our bodies back onto the bed, causing Mila's body to tuck underneath mine. I waste no time taking her mouth with mine. With our mouths fighting a never-ending battle, Mila's body seeks friction as her hips buck, and her wet pussy finds my aching cock. Pressing my hips into her center, I slide my cock back and forth through her wet slit. Breaking our kiss, she starts to beg.

"Reid, please, I need more." Raking her nails up my back, she pleads once more, "Reid, I need you."

Fuck, she had to go on and say the one last thing sure to break me. She needs me. Not this, me. Resting my forehead on hers, I give her something I have never given another woman. "I love you, Mila." Shocked at my confession, she sucks in a breath. Seeing the truth in my eyes, she palms my cheek. "I love you too, Reid."

With nothing else left to say, I reach between us and take my cock in my hand, placing the head at her entrance. I take both of Mila's hands in mine and bring them above our heads and link our fingers together. With our eyes locked on one another, I thrust forward, taking the woman I love entirely, making her mine in every way. Kissing her neck, I still for a moment letting Mila become accustomed to my size because she is so fucking tight. "You okay, baby?"

"Yes," she whispers and then groans when I swivel my hips.

"So fuckin' good, Kitten. So perfect," I praise, picking up my pace.

"Oh God, Reid, I'm going to come." When I feel her pussy begin to flutter around my cock, I move my head down and take her nipple into my mouth and suck. Seconds later, her pussy spasms around me like a vise as her orgasm crashes over her, and my name on her lips has me thrusting one last time before planting myself deep inside of her as I chase my release.

With Mila sleeping upstairs in my bed, I decided to come down to my office and get to work on finding out about her parents. After I have tapped into River's system, I find their motive to get their daughter out of the picture. "Son of a bitch," I mutter. I almost don't believe what I am looking at, but sure enough, Mila's grandmother has Mila as the beneficiary of her will. And in the event of her death, Mila will inherit 2.5 million dollars. Mila's grandfather purchased some stocks in the '50s. He left everything to his wife Charlotte, Mila's grandmother, and she has left everything to Mila.

No way does Mila know anything about this. She would have told me. I have no idea why her grandmother never told her, but my guess is that she didn't want Mila's parents to find out. It looks like they found out alright. There is no other reason for them wanting their daughter and granddaughter dead. Now I need to find out why the hell they would go through such drastic measures for this money. From the way Mila talks, her parents are wealthy. Thirty minutes later, I have my answer. The Vaughn's are tapped out. As in flat on their ass broke. Too many bad investments by Mila's father. And his credit card receipts are showing some extramarital activities Mrs. Vaughn would not like. A perfect example of you can't judge a book by its cover. On the outside, these two are well-respected, upstanding citizens. On the inside, they are liars and cheaters, the lowest of the fucking low.

I get to work setting things in motion. Contacting the right people to eliminate the situation and put her parents where they belong. Picking up my phone, I find the name I'm looking for and wait for Jake to answer. It's nearly midnight, but Prez knows I wouldn't call at this time unless it were necessary. He answers after two rings, "Son?"

"Can we have a sit down in the morning, Prez," I ask.

"You got it."

These motherfuckers don't know what low is, but they sure are about to find out.

# 16

## MILA

W aking up to an empty bed this morning was a little disappointing but not at all surprising. If I had to guess, I'd say Reid is downstairs in his office.

Swinging my legs over the side of Reid's bed, I stretch my arms above my head and let the blanket fall from around my body. The delicious ache between my legs instantly reminds me of last night. A smile tugs at my face at the memory. I shocked myself with how bold and confident I had been.

"That's a sight I could get used to seeing every mornin'."

Looking over my shoulder, I see Reid standing in the doorway of his room with a look of pure desire on his face. Raking my gaze up and down his body, I admire his toned body. From the athletic shorts sitting low on his hips, to his broad chest, to the tattoos covering his arm, all the way up to his freshly shaven head. "Yeah, I think I could say the same thing," I tell him as I stand and snag his shirt off the floor. I make it a point to turn toward him and slowly slip it on over my head.

Reid swiftly strides toward me. My breath catches when he hooks his arm around my waist, forcing me to take several steps back until my body is pressed against the wall, and his mouth claims mine. Through my drunken, lust filled haze, my body is working purely on instinct. When he grabs my ass and lifts my body off the floor, I wrap my legs around his lean, firm hips. Reid shifts his weight and reaches between our fussed bodies, releasing his cock from the confines of his shorts. The feel of his fingers gliding over my pussy to test my readiness causes a whimper to leave my lips.

"So fuckin' wet for me," Reid's rough voice growls into my ear.

*I'm always ready for him.*

Before I can process another thought, I feel his hard shaft surge in, and throw my head back with a cry of pure bliss.

"Look at me, Kitten," he demands, keeping a steady rhythm.

Reid is drilling into me hard and fast, and I love it.

"You keep your eyes on me when you come," he commands.

The primal sound of our heavy breathing is fueling my impending orgasm. It's hitting me hard and fast, just like the fucking Reid is delivering. My brain is too far gone. The way our bodies are joined together is so good and so overpowering I have trouble obeying his demand to keep my eyes open.

"Come with me, Kitten."

*I do.*

I don't remember when he rid me of my shirt, but I come with Reid's sweaty chest rubbing against my bare breasts. I come with his thick cock deep inside of me, filling me with his release. I come with his fist in my hair, demanding control. Lastly, I come with his name on my lips.

"This is another thing I could get used to," Reid announces from his seat at the kitchen table.

"What's that?" I ask coyly.

"You in my kitchen cookin'."

Rising from his chair, he makes his way toward me, where I am standing in front of the stove and wraps his strong arms around me from behind.

"You belong here, Mila, you and Ava. I want my girls back home where they belong." The hand I am using to flip pancakes freezes. One of Reid's arms leaves my body as he reaches out and turns off the stove before he urges me to turn and face him. "Tell me what you're thinkin', babe."

I swallow past the knot in my throat, "Do you mean it? Do you really want us here? You have to understand what you're asking, Reid. You saw what it's like having a little kid living here."

"I know what I'm asking, Mila. I miss my girls. I wouldn't have said something unless I was sure. I know what I want, and I want you, and I want Ava too." Placing his hands on either side of my face, he steals a kiss and continues. "How about a trial run? You and Ava stay here until we figure out what's going on with your situation. Once things have settled, we can revisit the subject."

"I think I can handle that," I tell him, accepting his offer. Living with Reid feels like home, and I feel safe. My primary concern is keeping my daughter safe. After what happened at the motel, I won't risk putting mine or Ava's lives in danger.

"I know what you're thinkin', Kitten. Your thoughts are playing out all over your beautiful face. I promise I won't let anything happen to you or Ava. I'll kill any motherfucker who dares to put their hands on you again." Reid's voice drips with venom and with promise. He kisses my forehead, "Come on, babe. Let's eat. Bella and Austin will be here soon to go with you to your house so you can pick up some things, and I need to head to the clubhouse to talk with Jake."

Putting my trust in him, I decide I'm going to let Reid do what he needs to do.

. . .

BELLA and I are sitting in the back seat of Austin's truck on our way to my Grams' house, where she doesn't waste any time asking me questions. "So, you and Ava are moving in with Reid?"

"Five minutes, Bella. Couldn't you wait five minutes?" I giggle.

"Shut up, and spill! You know I'm dying over here," she jests, nudging me in my side with her elbow.

"Yes, we're moving in. He wants to keep us safe until the dust with my parents settles. He also admitted he misses us and wants Ava and me to live with him long term, but I only agreed on a trial basis. I don't think Reid fully understands what he will be getting himself into when it comes to living with a child. Sure, he got a taste the month we were there while I was his nurse, but I believe he needs more time to be sure."

"Oh, he's sure. If it's one thing I know for certain about The Kings' men, is when they want something, they get it. Reid wouldn't have suggested you living with him if he wasn't one hundred percent sure. The 'trial run' makes you feel better moving forward."

"Reid said the same thing to me this morning," I sigh. "Maybe, I'm trying to play it smart. You know? I have a daughter who is already attached to him. This whole thing with Reid seems too good to be true. I have always taken care of myself, and now he insists I let him do it." I gaze out the window and watch the clouds roll by, "He hasn't asked me about her biological father, or if he was even in the picture. When I confessed weeks ago she was the product of a one-night stand he didn't blink an eye. There was no disgusted look or judgment from him," I admit.

"Hold on a minute." Bella interrupts. "Why would anyone have reason to judge you for having a one-night stand?"

I shrug my shoulders and look down at my lap, "I don't know. I guess I'm a little embarrassed. It didn't help my parents made it a point to call me a tramp, and tell me how stupid I was to allow myself to get pregnant."

"Mila, you listen to me. You have nothing to be ashamed of. Ava is a gift. Anyone would be lucky to have both of you. Reid can see that. He can see how special you are. I'm sorry your parents can't see what everyone else does." Taking my hand in hers, I look at Bella when she speaks her next words. "Anyone who chooses not to see what an amazing, special, and caring person you are is not worth having in your life. It's their loss, Mila."

In keeping with the theme of spilling my guts, I make another confession, "I'm in love with him."

"I know you are. Reid is in love with you too."

"Don't you think it's a little soon?" I ask her.

"Says who? Love is love, Mila. Love is timeless and has no boundaries. It doesn't matter if you fall in love in a day, a week, a month, or even a year. All that matters is it feels right, and you are happy. Life is too short. When you find love and happiness, I say, grab hold of it and never let go."

"How did you get to be so smart?" I ask my friend.

"Life. You live, and you learn."

"That's the truth," I sigh. "You're a good friend, Bella. The best. I don't know what I'd do without you," I tell her while leaning over and hugging her. A throat clearing from the front seat breaks mine and Bella's moment.

"Uh, sorry to interrupt ladies, but we're here," Austin tells us.

Climbing out of his truck, I notice a car parked in Grams' driveway. On closer inspection, it looks to be a rental, and I know who it is.

"Whose car?" Bella inquires.

My blood begins to boil as I storm across the lawn in the direction of the front door. "My parents," I say without stopping. How dare they show up here. I notice Austin jogging to catch up with me.

"Mila, wait. Let me go in first," Austin interjects.

"No. Fuck that. I'm not scared of them. What I am is sick of their shit." Stepping from around Austin, I burst through the front door.

"Shit. Why don't women ever fuckin' listen?" Austin curses from behind me. I see him reach into his cut and pull out his cell phone. One guess as to who he's calling. Regardless, I'm going to have words with my parents. When I look behind me, Bella is hot on my trail and looks just as pissed as I am.

Having heard a commotion, Richard and Susan Vaughn both round the corner of the hallway at the same time as me, and I nearly collide with my mother. I'm a little taken aback at my mother's appearance. She looks out of sorts. Her clothes are rumpled, and her hair is a mess. My father is looking much the same.

"How the hell did you get here?" I demand.

"Your grandmother hasn't changed the locks in over fifteen years," my mother scoffs. "I used my old key. I didn't break in. But seeing as this house will soon belong to me, it doesn't make much of a difference now does it."

When I have it in mind to wipe the smug-ass look off her face, I hear the rumble of several bikes, and I offer a smug smile of my own because I know my man is about to walk through the door.

## 17

## REID

"Hey, brother. How's Mila holdin' up?" Quinn inquires as I stride into the clubhouse. "Doing' good," I say as I walk over to the bar where Logan is sitting.

"Hey, what's up? I wasn't expecting to see anyone out here today," I mention as I take a seat and wait for Prez to show.

"Well, since my woman is with yours, and Gabriel's woman has the kids at the park, we thought we'd drag our asses out here for a few hours and shoot the shit, maybe go out back and do some target practice," he says taking a drag from his cigarette. "You wanna join us?" he questions.

"Got a sit-down with Jake," I inform Logan.

"Anything we can help you with?" I hear Gabriel's voice from across the room where he's sitting on the couch. I twist in my seat to look at him. "Nah, man. Found some dirt on Mila's parents. Just letting him know what's up."

"You finally stakin' your claim on her?" Prez asks as the front door slams behind him.

"Forever, brother," I tell him.

"Alright. Let's get down to business." Jake motions for me to follow him to his office. Pulling out the chair, I take a seat and wait for him to take his before talking.

Under normal circumstances, I wouldn't have brought anyone else in on personal shit like this, but the fact that we may have to rub elbows with the law again means I need to make Jake aware of my findings and my plans. The little information I gave him over the phone last night was just the tip of the iceberg. The deeper I dug, the more I found. "I need to make you aware of the fact that Mila's parents are being investigated for embezzlement on a federal level, which means I may have to deal with the law directly myself to fix the problems they've been causing her lately," I explain.

"You plan on handin' them over?" Prez asks, crossing his arms over his chest.

"I happened to find what the federal government couldn't," I lean back in my chair, "which is all the evidence they need to put the Vaughn's behind bars for the next ten years." I'm not going to tell him about the will or the money. None of that information has any effect on why the club needs to know what's going on. Before I continue, my phone rings. I usually wouldn't answer a call during a sit-down, but with what just went down with Mila, I won't take any chances. I dig the phone out of the pocket of my cut and immediately notice Austin's number lighting up the screen. My stomach sinks. Swiping, I answer my phone. "Yeah."

"Reid, we got trouble over here. Mila's parents are inside. Mind hoppin' on that bike off yours and getting over here before the neighbors decide to call the cops?"

I hang up and stick my phone back into my pocket. The look on my face prompts Jake to stand.

"Trouble?" Prez asks as he steps forward with fists balled at his sides.

"Yeah, Mila and Bella went to her old place to pack a few things. Sorry, Prez, I gotta ride." I turn to leave.

"You'll fall in behind me, son. We'll all ride," he orders.

Five strong, we mount our bikes and take off toward Mila's.

With the rumble of our Harleys rolling through the neighborhood, people stop and stare. One by one, we pull into her driveway blocking the cars already sitting there. No one is leaving until we're damn good and ready for them to.

Dismounting my bike, I stride toward the front door where Austin is standing with his arms crossed. Stepping to the side, he clears the way, and one by one, my brothers fall in behind me, and in a matter of seconds, the small living room is ass to elbow full of bikers. I step up beside Mila and place myself between her and her petrified looking parents.

"I see you associate with gang members now," her mother snubs as she glances around the room.

"Look, you plastic ass bi—" Bella starts to mouth off before Logan cuts her off by grabbing her around the waist, pulling her off to the side.

"We got a fuckin' problem," I bark, leveling my gaze at Mila's father.

Standing taller, her father puffs his chest out, "I'd say we do. You're trespassing."

"Like hell I am. This is my home," Mila says, standing her ground. On paper, it appears that they legally have the right to be here as their names are on the deed to the home. But I'm willing to bet that piece of paper was forged just like all the rest.

Making a sudden move, her father reaches for the inside of his suit jacket. On instinct, I pull my weapon from the inside of my cut, "Don't you fuckin' move another inch," I warn him. Visibly gulping as he stares down the barrel I have pointed at his face, I reach inside his coat only to retrieve a phone. Dumb son of a bitch almost got himself killed, making a move like that in a room full of bikers. "Plannin' on callin' the cops?" I ask lowering my gun.

"You're on my property." He crosses his arms, trying his best not to show how nervous he is, but the beads of sweat forming on his brow and upper lip say different. I'd say he's about ready to shit his pants, not knowing what will happen next. As much as I want to fuck with him a little, I decide against it. I need them to think they have the upper hand with Mila, for now. The less fight, the less suspecting they will be when the storm rolls in.

"She's gonna get what she wants, and then we'll be on our way," I inform them.

"She can't have anything that belongs to my mother. Not one thing. She can only take what belongs to her and that child of hers," her mother speaks up in a disgusted tone. My blood boils at the way she says *that child*. I have to keep telling myself now is not the time.

"She never meant anything to you. You have no right to—"

I pivot and face Mila, interrupting her mid-rant and grab her face in my hands, "Go get what you need for you and Ava," I say, giving her a look urging her to trust me. Seeming to understand what I need from her, she steps around me. Her along with Bella, Logan, and Austin walk toward the hallway and disappear into a room. "I'm sure you don't mind giving them some time to gather clothes and such, so go ahead and take a seat. As soon as my brothers have the truck loaded we'll leave," I tell them.

For the better part of thirty minutes, the guys load the back of Austin's truck. Without looking back, we leave her parents speechless in the living room, and I head home with Mila on the back of my bike.

The guys all stuck around and unloaded the truck getting everything inside before heading out, but not before I thanked them for having my back today. Walking up to Mila, I wrap my arms around her waist, rest my chin on her head and stand staring out the large windows facing the town skyline with her. "Come sit down on the couch. I need to talk to you."

Dropping my hand, I take hers, and we walk to the couch. As

soon as my ass hits the cushion, Mila turns to face me. "I'm sorry I'm causing so much trouble."

"Babe, none of this is your fault. We don't get to choose who we're born to. My dad was a great fuckin' man, but my mom...let's just say she was no mother of the year," I tell her. I'm surprised I said anything about my mom. I never talk about her to anyone. "Listen, I dug around in your parent's past and their present. I'm talking about everything. Babe, they are flat-ass broke. Lots of bad investments."

Shifting her body to face me, she pulls her legs up on the couch and crosses them. "Broke? I don't see how they can be broke. Reid, my parents have always had money," she tells me.

"They're also being investigated on embezzlement and fraud, Kitten. They've stolen money from a shit ton of their clients over the past fifteen years."

Fidgeting, Mila gets off the couch and starts pacing the floor. I sit quietly for a couple of minutes, giving her some time before dumping more on her.

Still pacing, she makes the statement, "There's more, isn't there? I've always known my parents were rotten apples, but that doesn't explain why suddenly they want to cause havoc in mine and Grams lives now."

Running my hands through my hair, I sigh. I'm about to drop the motherload of news on her. "They're after your grandmother's money."

Her pacing stops, and her face loses all expressions, "What money? Grams has been living off widow's benefits for years now." She sits back down this time on the arm of the couch next to me.

"Your grandfather made some investments that started to pay off after his death, babe. And it's still drawing interest. Your Grams was beneficiary to that money. She's had over two million dollars sitting in a bank account she may have never known about, or she's forgotten. Unfortunately, I believe your parents found out," I explain.

Staring blankly, Mila says nothing. I wrap an arm around her waist and pull her into my lap. A couple of tears fall from her beautiful face. "Kitten, your grams has a will. In the event she passes, everything she owns goes to you and Ava. Everything," I finish telling her.

"And that's why my parents wanted me out of the picture," she pieces it all together. With nothing more to do, I hold her hoping it's enough to comfort her. We sit in silence for I don't know how long, but long enough to watch the evening sun start to creep across the hardwood floors.

"What's the plan? I have a court hearing tomorrow. How will I prove all this to the judge?" she asks with worry and defeat.

"I need you to give that lawyer friend of yours a call. I have a plan, but I need his help," I inform her. The chances of him helping are a long shot, but it's one we need to take. I don't need my name associated with anything I'll be handing over. Not just for my sake, but the club's as well.

"Now?" Mila asks after grabbing hold of my hand.

"Now, Kitten. What I have planned needs to happen tomorrow, so we have to act fast." Without hesitation, she gets up and retrieves her phone. I listen to her speak with him. She doesn't go into detail only that she could use his help pertaining to court tomorrow. After ending the call, she slips her phone into the back pocket of her jeans. "He has time for us now."

That was all I needed to hear.

It being the weekend, we make our way toward his house. We took Mila's car, knowing we'd be swinging by Alba's on the way home to pick up Ava. I glance over at Mila. She's been silent for the whole ride. I'm sure she is wrapping her head around the information overload I dumped on her at home. I reach over and place my hand on her thigh giving it a light squeeze, "You okay?"

Pulling up to the address she provided me, I cut off the engine and wait for her to answer me, but her spaced look tells me she didn't hear a word I said. "Kitten," I speak a little louder with a firmer tone. She turns her head, and her weary eyes connect with mine. "I'm sorry. What did you say?"

Shit, I hate seeing her drowning in all this bullshit. "You okay?" I ask her again.

"Yeah. It's a lot to process, but I'm good. More tired than anything," she breathes.

"You ready to go in?" I motion with my head toward River's house. Nodding her answer, she exits the car, and we make our way up to the front door. After rapping my knuckles a few times, the door swings open with River standing on the other side. His eyes land on Mila, briefly causing my hand to clench at my side. "Come in," he says, stepping to the side.

As soon as we step in fully, a little redheaded girl comes skipping toward us.

"Ava!" she squeals.

Mila looks down at her with a sad smile. "Oh, I'm sorry, Willow, but I don't have Ava with me this time." Disappointment spread over her little freckled-faced as she hangs her head.

"You'll get to see her tomorrow at preschool, pumpkin." River kneels and lifts her sad face to look at his.

"Okay," she softly whispers to her father.

"Go play in your room for a little bit, pumpkin. I need to talk to Mila and her friend."

After she's gone, River stands and turns, then extends his hand toward me, and we shake. "Mr. Carter," he says.

"You can call me Reid," I tell him.

"Why don't you two have a seat in the living room? I'll get us something to drink. Beer, okay?"

"A beer sounds good. Thanks," I tell him.

Disappearing into the kitchen, he returns, holding three

bottles in his hands along with a couple of cold bottles of water. I take his offer and let a couple gulps slide down my throat.

"Alright," River says, taking a seat in his recliner. "What can I help with?" He looks directly at me, waiting for the answer to his question. Mila looks at me as well and waits. She's giving me the lead. Trusting me.

"Have some evidence that found its way to me, which needs to get in the hands of the proper authorities before the court hearing tomorrow. Can you make that happen?" I eye him taking another swig of my beer.

"You need to remain anonymous?" he asks, taking a pull from his own bottle.

"All I want is for her parents to be in cuffs tomorrow."

"I can do that. Send me what you have, and I'll take care of it," he's quick to respond. Mila is sitting beside me on the couch, nursing her beer, and her knee is bouncing with pent up nerves. I know she wants answers. Answers I can't give her.

"Mila," he leans forward in his chair and gets her attention, "make sure you're about ten minutes early getting to the courthouse tomorrow. I'll already be there waiting for you. Both of you," he looks from her to me, then back at her.

We stay a few more minutes while River goes over what to expect in the morning before leaving. Once he's finished going over all the ins and outs of what to expect, I take Mila's drink from her before pulling her to stand. I wrap my arm around her waist and lean in, kissing her temple, "Come on, Kitten. Let's get Ava and go home."

# 18

## MILA

Reid and I are driving to the nursing home to visit with Grams. I told him I wanted to see her before going to court this morning. Alba offered to keep Ava for another night since I had court. I spoke to my baby girl briefly on the phone, and she didn't need convincing to stay another night. Bella said she would go to her sister's house this morning and pick Ava up and take her to preschool. I honestly don't know what I would do without my friends. Bella and Alba have gone above and beyond with their help.

If my parents get their way today, I fear they will cut off my visitation with my grandmother. This will also be the first time Reid is meeting her. I'm not nervous because my Grams has never been one to judge others. She won't let his looks or his cut hold any bearing on the kind of man he is. As we walk down the halls of the home, we stop at the nurse's station and are greeted by Joni.

"Hey, sweetheart, how are you? And who is this handsome young man?" she asks.

"Hi, Joni," I adjust my purse hanging on my shoulder, "I'm

good, and this is my...Reid." I've never had an actual boyfriend, and the word feels foreign, just thinking about it.

"I see. It's about time you got yourself a man, girly and looks like you have a strapping one at that. I bet he's taking good care, you, honey."

Oh, my God. I feel my face flame at Joni's words, and when I look at Reid, he's sporting a smug grin on his face.

"Oh, honey, don't be embarrassed, why if I were twenty years younger..." she trails off as I cut in.

"Joni!" After she and Reid have a good chuckle at my expense, I decide to change the subject. "How's Grams doing today?"

"She's doing wonderful. Today is a good day," Joni chirps.

Walking into my grandmother's room, I spot her sitting in her chair next to the window, and her attention is on the television where she is watching the morning news.

"Mila," she greets warmly and with a smile when she sees me walking toward her.

"Hi, Grams. I brought someone for you to meet." When she notices Reid standing behind me, her smile grows.

"Well, move out of the way, dear, so I can meet him." I love that my Grams still has some sass. "And what's your name young man?"

"I'm Reid; it's nice to finally meet you, ma'am. My girl has told me so much about you," he introduces himself taking my grandmother's hand and kissing the back of it.

"Looks and charm. You hit the jackpot with this one, Mila," Grams says. "Tell me something young man, are you taking good care of my granddaughter?"

"Grams, how do you know we're together, he could just be a friend."

"I may be an old woman, Mila, but I'm not stupid. I see it in your eyes and his as well. You're more than friends. Am I right?" she asks, quirking her eyebrow, and it's Reid that answers.

"You would be correct, ma'am. Mila is mine, and so is Ava. I plan on taking care of them both."

Over the next couple of hours, Reid and I continue to sit and talk with Grams, and she even talks him into playing a couple of games of cards. I fall deeper in love with the man as I watch him interact with the woman who means the world to me. When it is finally time to leave, I watch as Grams ushers Reid forward for a hug, and I don't miss her whispering something into his ear before he then looks at her with a warm smile and nods his head. *I wonder what that was about.*

"Thank you for being so kind to my grandmother," I tell Reid on our way out of the nursing home. Stopping in front of his bike, he turns to me and grabs my hips bringing me closer to him.

"No need to thank me, Kitten. She's important to you, so she's important to me." Encircling my arms around his waist, I lay my head on his chest.

"You're too good to me. How did I get so lucky?"

Reid rests his cheek on top of my head, "I'm the lucky one, babe."

Riding on the back of Reid's bike on the way to the courthouse, my nerves are a jumbled mess. Reid has assured me that everything will work out, but my parents are ruthless lawyers. I've witnessed them in court a handful of times growing up. I can only hope the judge today is not impressed with the Vaughn's and their reputation.

As Reid turns the corner and the courthouse comes into view, I become overwhelmed at the sight ahead of us. Parked in front of the building is a row of at least fifteen bikes, and the thing that stands out the most are the men wearing cuts. Reid's brothers; his family. When Reid parks his motorcycle next to Jake's, I unfold myself from his back and climb off.

"Prez," Reid acknowledges Jake with a nod.

"What is everyone doing here?" I ask no one in particular, and it's Jake, the man Reid calls his President, who answers my question.

"You belong to Reid; therefore, you belong to the club. You're family now, and we take care of our own. That includes our support." Looking around at the men standing in front of me, I see Logan, Gabriel, Quinn, Doc, Austin, Blake, and several other club members. None of these men know me very well, yet here they are.

"Thank you," I manage to choke out past my sudden overwhelming emotion.

"Come on, Kitten," Reid's gentle voice whispers into the shell of my ear as he pulls me to his side and leads me into the courthouse. Across the lobby, we spot River talking to a man in a suit who looks to be in his early thirties.

"That's the lead investigator. The one I was telling you about. He and his partner flew in from New York as soon as River contacted them," Reid informs me just before we step up to the man in question.

"Special Agent Holden, this is Mila Vaughn and Reid Carter," River introduces us both. Reid and I both shake hands with him, but it is Reid who speaks first.

"We appreciate you coming all this way on such short notice."

By the look on Agent Holden's face after taking in Reid's cut and then looking over our shoulders and through the window of the courthouse at the slew of bikers outside, I can sense he's not sure what to make of us.

"So, what's the plan?" I asked, breaking the tension.

"We're waiting for the Vaughn's to show. Once they do, they'll be taken into custody. I've already spoken to the judge. In lieu of the findings against your parents, the judge has decided to drop your case and the suit they have against you. The situation is pretty cut and dry. Evidence shows Richard and Susan Vaughn came after you out of desperation," Agent Holden tells us.

"See, Kitten; I told you I'd take care of everything. "

Letting out a deep breath of relief, I feel all the tension my body was holding hostage, leave. "So, that's it? Just like that?" I ask, needing final clarification. This time it is Reid who answers.

"Yeah, babe, it's over. Your parents can't hurt you, Ava, or Grams anymore."

No sooner do those words leave Reid's lips when a frantic Bella comes rushing through the doors of the lobby with a wild looking Logan on her heels. From the moment Bella's eyes meet mine, I know the statement Reid just made couldn't be farther from the truth. I know in my gut what Bella is about to tell me is going to fuck me up. I can feel it with everything I am. So, when my friend rushes up to me with a tear-streaked face and the look of horror in her eyes, she delivers the blow. Two words, that's all it takes to bring my world crashing down.

"Ava's missing."

And there it is, because my daughter is my world, my reason for being. From this moment, everything happens in slow motion.

"What the fuck you talkin' about Ava's missing?!" Reid shouts. "She's at preschool."

Frantically shaking her head back and forth while having a death grip on her phone, Bella explains. "I just got a call from them. They said they tried calling Mila first, but her phone kept going straight to voicemail, so they called me since I'm one of Ava's emergency contacts. Mrs. Sarah said the new girl they hired let her grandparent pick her up."

I feel my gut twisting with every word leaving Bella's mouth.

"What do you mean, her grandparent? They can't just release a child to just anybody."

I don't try to stick around and wait for Reid to finish his statement. I've heard all I need to, and now I'm going to find my daughter. Because of some incompetent moron, my baby is in the hands of evil. My parents. The same parents who didn't give a second thought to hiring someone to kill their daughter.

On autopilot, I turn away from Bella and Reid and start sprinting across the lobby of the courthouse and out the door. I faintly hear Reid calling out my name behind me. Reaching the sidewalk, I come to a complete stop as I realize I haven't a clue as to what to do or where to even start when it comes to finding my daughter.

"Mila, baby, look at me," Reid coaxes with both his hands cupping my face. It's at that moment with his face a breath away from mine that I suddenly snap out of my fog.

"I don't know what to do," I admit in an almost robotic voice I don't recognize. Latching on to Reid's cut, I repeat myself; only this time when the words leave my mouth, I feel my legs give out from underneath me. "My baby is gone, Reid, and I don't know what to do. What do I do?" I wail at the same time I'm lifted into Reid's strong arms.

The next thing I know, I'm being placed in the front seat of Bella's car. "Bella is taking you back to the clubhouse. I want you to stay there. Blake and Austin are going to follow behind," Reid orders. "Look at me, baby." When I do, I see nothing but fierceness and determination on his face. "I'm going to bring her back to you. You have my word."

With his parting words, Reid shuts the car door and walks back toward his brothers, who, through my clouded vision, I see mounting their bikes as Jake shouts his orders. With Bella driving in the direction of the clubhouse, I watch helplessly as Reid's tail lights disappear in the opposite direction.

## 19

## REID

I hated leaving Mila in the state she was in, but I need to find Ava. I'm not sure how they got tipped off to the fact that the feds were waiting to arrest them. I suppose they haven't gone this many years doing what they've been doing, not to know how to keep a step ahead of the law in some form or fashion, but kidnapping their granddaughter is desperate and low.

I don't know what their endgame is by taking Ava, but without a doubt, I know what ours would be if it weren't for the fact that the law is out looking for them as well. In a matter of minutes, this town will be on lockdown. The Kings may be a sorted bunch, but one thing you don't fuck with is family—our family. The feds tried pushing their weight around, but they should know demanding a bunch of bikers to stay out of it was not going to fly. They have their way of doing things, and we have ours. All of us have a common goal, and that's finding Mila's daughter.

After searching with the rest of the guys and coming up empty, I decided to come back to my place, and doing some digging would turn up a clue to where they might have gone after leaving the preschool, but it hasn't done a damn bit of good.

"Fuck!" I roar, slamming my laptop closed. Prez has several of the guys on the roads looking for the car they were last seen in while I try to trace down their whereabouts by looking up any recent credit card activity. I've found nothing. Nothing because all known accounts belonging to the Vaughn's were frozen. Where the fuck could they have gone with no financial means to get there? I get up and pace the floors. I stop and let my head fall back and look up at the ceiling, letting out a frustrated breath. *Fuckin' think,* I chastise myself.

Deciding to get back on my bike, I turn around to grab my key from the top of my desk. I pause a moment to stare at a picture of my brother and me standing side by side. The photo was taken the day I earned my cut and sitting to the right of the frame is Ava's teddy bear. The one she gave me to hold on to, hoping it would make me feel better. Picking the toy up, I study it. A moment of clarity hits me. I can't explain it, but I know where she is. With the bear in my hand, I get to my bike as quickly as I can. Before I turn the engine over, I tuck her teddy securely inside the bike's left side saddlebag.

Fifteen minutes later, I cut my engine and let my bike coast, stopping two houses down from Mila's Grams. With all the chaos, no one thought to come here including me. As soon as I swing my leg over, getting off, I hear a vehicle pulling up behind me. Looking over my shoulder, I watch Officer Jenkins stop and open his car door. *Shit.* I should have known they'd have someone with a badge try and follow us around.

Apparently, waiting for me to let him in on the reason why I'm here, I clue him in. Only because I don't want to take the chance on fuckin' anything up. "If my hunch is correct," I lift my hand and point toward the house, "they have Ava in there."

"I need to call it in," he informs me.

He can do what he wants, but I'm not waiting to find out. I turn my back to him, walking toward the house.

"Mr. Carter!" he calls out. Pausing, I give him a chance to finish.

"Remember, there may be a four-year-old child in there, so act accordingly."

I'll take whatever measures are needed to make sure she stays safe. I don't say a word. While Officer Jenkins mumbles a 'Goddamnit' and calls in our location over the police radio, I keep walking.

Intent on answers, I carefully make my way to the front door with a purpose. Checking the knob, I turn it. Surprisingly, it isn't locked. Not taking the risk of Ava seeing me with a gun, I keep it inside my cut. She was just taken by two people she has never met before. By desperate people—people who even though she is their own flesh and blood have proven family means nothing to them.

Slowly, I make my way inside. Not wanting any surprises to spring up behind me, I close the door. Upon glancing around the living room, there are no signs anyone has been here since yesterday, so I cautiously take my time crossing the room. That's when I hear it. A soft little giggle. Ava's little laugh is coming from down the hall. The further I get down the short hallway, the clearer the sound gets. I stop right outside Ava's bedroom door and listen.

Holding my breath, I open the door. Sitting on her bed next to Mila's mother is Ava. Bouncing off the bed with excitement as if nothing is wrong, Ava skips toward me, and I scoop her up into my awaiting arms. She may not be anything to me by blood, but I feel she is every bit mine and I will protect her. While I hug her, Mila's mother watches on with a muted stare. As if she's longing for something that's just within her reach, but she can't touch it. The distant sounds of sirens fill the air alerting both of us to the nearby presence of the police.

"She is a sweet little girl," Mrs. Vaughn murmurs.

I narrow my eyes at her. "Where's your husband?" I ask her.

She drops her shoulder and turns her head to peer out the window to her right. "Took off."

"Why? Why her daughter?" I ask her.

Dropping her gaze to her lap, she wrings her hands together. "We stayed here last night. No money, nowhere to go, and just before court this morning, Robert said he would be right back. When he returned, he had Ava with him. I know I'm a lot of things, Mr. Carter. I know I haven't been a good mother, but he wanted to use her as a bargaining chip, and I couldn't go along with it. So, he left. Took the car and left us here." She looks at Ava, who I still have in my arms. I can tell she wants to say more when we hear the blaring sirens outside the house and the sound of multiple car doors slamming. I recognize a voice belonging to Officer Jenkins making his presence known as he enters the home. I continue to keep my eyes fixed on Mrs. Vaughn and listen as the officers' weighty feet approach the bedroom from behind me.

"Carter," Jenkins states in an even tone. Most likely so he doesn't alarm and upset Ava. "I'll take it from here. Her mother is waiting outside."

Before I leave the room, I speak one more time to Mila's mother. Lowering my voice, I tell her, "You will never lay eyes on these two again."

As I'm emerging from the hall and entering the living room, Mila breaks past the other officer standing near the front door. When she sees I have Ava safe and unharmed with her little arms draped around my neck, she loses it all over again. Desperately trying to hold her emotions in, she reaches for her daughter, and I place her into her mama's arms. I watch as they embrace one another. Pulling both into me, I hold them.

"Babe," I lift Mila's chin, and she looks up, meeting my eyes, "they'll be leading your mother out soon. You wanna take off?" I ask her while running my fingers through her hair, pushing the few fallen pieces from around her face, as I peer down at her.

"Take us home," she tells me.

The three of us walk outside to find an awaiting Bella standing next to her car. Tears start to stream down her face the moment she lays eyes on Mila holding Ava. Quickly wiping them away, she smiles as we approach. "Bella, take them home. Give me a minute, and I'll be right behind you," I inform her. I wait until all three of them are safely inside the car and buckled in before retrieving my bike a couple of houses down.

When I pass Agent Holden, the federal agent in charge of the whole investigation of the Vaughns, stops me with and extends his hand. "Thank you," he acknowledges and shakes my hand. I give him a firm nod in response before we both go our separate ways.

My phone ringing in my pocket causes my pace to slow as I dig it out. Looking at the lit-up screen, I see Gabriel's number and swipe to answer. "What you got, brother?"

"We found the father thirty minutes outside of town. His dumb ass ran out of gas and had nowhere to go. What do you want done with him, brother?" Gabriel's utters.

He kidnapped a little girl. My family. I'm sure my other brother would agree he has a little justice coming to him. "Rough him up a little. Nothing major. He needs to be turned over to the authorities alive and in one piece," I tell Gabriel, but silence hangs in the air instead of a response. I smirk, knowing I soiled his plans to have a little fun. The man is as loyal to his family as they come. Gabriel takes shit like this personally. "Sorry, brother. Not this time."

"You got it," his gruff voice says before hanging up. The motherfucker picked the wrong town and the wrong family to mess with. He is damn lucky to be receiving a busted lip or some bruised ribs. In any other circumstances, he would have a date with death.

Getting on my bike, I roll up behind Bella's car to bring up the rear, and we head home.

## 20

# MILA

It's been twenty-four hours since Reid placed Ava back in my arms, and in those twenty-four hours, I'm grateful Ava was none the wiser as to what happened. I know she must have been scared when my father took her from preschool, but she doesn't seem to have any lasting effects. I'm finding it difficult to let her go. She even slept in the bed between Reid and me last night, snuggled right into my side.

My hope is when she gets older; this incident will be a forgotten memory. However, there is one last thing I need to do before I can completely put my past behind me. I need to see my mother. I want—no, I need answers. It's time to close this chapter in my life and never look back. Once I do, I feel I'll be able to have the closure I need and move on with the rest of my life.

Reid mentioned last night both of my parents are to be taken back to New York tomorrow. So, it's now or never. Turning my attention away from my daughter, who is quietly playing with her toys on the living room floor, I look to Reid, who is sitting on the sofa next to me, his attention also on Ava. "I want to see my mother. You think you can make that happen for me?"

Without questioning me, he answers, "Yeah, babe. I'll make a call."

I love how he gets me without explaining. Somehow, he knows I need this, and I trust him to make it happen. While setting up visitation with my mother, Reid contacted my supervisor at the nursing home requesting personal time off due to a family emergency. When he came to me and announced what he had done, I was about to open my mouth and say something when he told me, "I thought you'd like to take the week off and spend it with Ava." Once he explained his reasoning, there was no way I could argue. A week home with my little girl sounded wonderful.

"Want me to get Bella or Alba to come to watch Ava while we go see your mom?" Reid asks.

"No, they've already done so much for me. I'm not going to ask any more of them. If it's alright with you, I'd rather go by myself."

"Hell no, Mila, you're not going by yourself. I don't want you confronting that bitch alone."

"You've got to stop acting like I'm made of glass. I'm going. I promise I can handle seeing her. It's time for me to put the past in the past so I can move on with my life. Confronting my mother is something I need to do alone. I need to show her she didn't win. I want her and my father to see they didn't break me," I explain with my voice steady and calm.

Letting out a sigh of defeat, Reid strides up to me standing toe to toe and cups my face. "You are the strongest, bravest woman I know."

Placing my hands on his forearms, I exhale. "Thank you," I say right before his lips meet mine, and I melt into him.

---

"ALRIGHT, Kitten, Agent Holden is expecting you down at the station. I'll stay here with Ava."

I give Reid one last kiss before walking over to Ava and kissing the top of her head. "Be good for Reid while I'm gone. Okay, sweetheart?"

"I will, Momma."

I almost don't want to leave the little bubble we've been in all day, but what I'm about to do I'm doing for the three of us. I can't move on and be the person or mother I want to be until I finally put the past behind me. Grabbing my car keys and purse off the kitchen counter, I make my way over to the door. With one last look over my shoulder, I glance at Reid. Nodding, he gives me the silent encouragement and strength I need.

Walking into the police station, I thought I would be more nervous, but what I feel is anger mixed with a little bit of sadness. I'm angry about everything my parents have done to my daughter and me, and sad because all I ever wanted from them was love and acceptance. "I'm here to see Agent Holden," I say to the officer behind the reception desk.

"What's your name?" he inquires.

As I am about to give the officer my name, Agent Holden appears from around the corner. "It's okay, Officer Jenkins, I've got it from here." Placing his hand on my back, he ushers me down the hall from where he came. "How are you holding up, Mila? How's Ava doing?"

"Ava's good. She doesn't seem to understand what happened, which I'm grateful for. As for me, I'm doing okay. This whole ordeal is a lot to process. I appreciate you allowing me to speak to my mother."

"Trust me, Mila; it's not a problem. I understand. We don't normally do things this way, but given the circumstances, I'm going to bend the rules. In my line of work, I see so many victims who don't get to see justice or get the closure they deserve."

"Does my mother know I'm coming to see her?" I question.

"Yes, and she agreed to meet with you. Our flight back to New York is in an hour, so I'm sorry you won't have much time."

"I don't need a lot of time. What I plan on saying to her will only take a minute."

"Alright. Reid said you only wanted to see your mother. What about your father? Do you wish to see him as well?"

I shake my head. "No, I have nothing to say to him."

Seeing the truth in my expression Agent Holden continues, "She is in the room behind you. I'll be right outside the door if you need me."

Seeing Susan Vaughn in a pair of handcuffs is surreal. I mean polished New York attorney Susan Vaughn, wife of Richard Vaughn and my mother. Through all my anger toward this woman, I'm surprised I'm still able to feel pity for her. That is what makes me so different from the woman in front of me. I have a heart. I feel compassion even for someone who played a part in trying to destroy my life; I still feel a twinge of sadness when looking at her and knowing she will be facing several years behind bars.

"You know, I was going to come in here and ask you why, but I've changed my mind. I already know why. You're a conniving bitch. You are a miserable excuse for a human being. Instead, I am going to tell you something about me. I am everything you're not. I'm a good mother. A loyal friend and an excellent nurse. Grams taught me all of those things. She showed me how to love, and when you love someone, you love them fiercely, faults and all. And because I refused to go along with what you and father wanted out of a daughter, you tossed me out like yesterday's garbage. But you know what?" I ask leaning forward and bracing my palms on the table in front of me and bringing my face closer to my mother's.

"You giving up on me was the best thing to ever happen to me. Moving to Polson and living with Grams was a blessing. I thrived and became the person I was always meant to be. It allowed me to follow my dreams of becoming a nurse and find the man who will one day be my husband. A man who, even though Ava is not his blood, loves her as if she were his daughter. A man who will teach her how a man should treat her by loving and respecting her mother. That is the kind of life I have. So, you see, you and father never stood a chance on ruining my life. You didn't break me. You made me stronger." By the time the last word leaves my mouth, I feel a weight lifted off my shoulders. I thought I wanted answers. Now I realize I didn't need them. I only needed my voice to be heard. Something I was never allowed growing up. Before my mother has a chance to respond, I turn on my heel and walk out the door, leaving my past behind me where it belongs.

---

SEVERAL WEEKS HAVE PASSED since the incident with my parents, and their names haven't been spoken of since. Reid, Ava, and I have fallen back into a routine with me going back to work. Reid has returned to doing what he loves, and that is getting his hands dirty on the job site. At his last PT session last week, he was cleared by the doctor to resume all normal activities.

As for Ava, she is no longer in preschool. During our week home together, I brought up the subject with Reid about switching preschools after what happened there with my father and the carelessness of the staff, I didn't feel comfortable sending her back. Now Ava spends her days with either Alba or Bella. The sisters showed up at Reid's place on a mission. When the pair suggested they take over babysitting duties, I knew Reid had a hand in the whole setup. I insisted they had already done enough for me and couldn't accept their offer. I was not one to take advantage of people's generosity. By the end of their visit, the three of us had worked out a schedule as to who would have Ava on what days. They said there was no reason for Ava to be in preschool when she has a family to look after her. I feel blessed to be a part of The Kings' family.

Some days Ava spends with Alba and baby Gabe, and a couple of days, she hangs with Bella at the garage. Those are the days my daughter comes home with a pocket full of cash, because "Uncle Quinn says lots of bad words." Yes, all of Reid's brothers have taken on the Uncle roles. Quinn's mouth alone is going to fund Ava's college tuition.

As for Grams, she is not doing so well. She caught a cold, and her body is slow to react to the antibiotics. When I stopped by this afternoon after work for my daily visit, the doctors informed me if she continues to worsen, they will be forced to admit her to the hospital. When I saw her today, she looked weak, and her skin was pale. My stomach clenched, and my heart ached at the sight of her lying in bed looking so small and frail. I'm not prepared to lose my Grams. There is a part of me that hates to see her suffering, but the selfish part of me wants her to hang on. I'd be lost without her. What would I do without her by my side? We have always been a team, her and me.

Even now, sitting beside her bed holding her hand, I will her to open her eyes and give me the answers. To tell me everything will be alright, just as she has done in the past. Resting my head on her bed while holding her hand, I close my eyes as tears roll down my cheeks because, at this moment, all I can do is pray.

Grams always said, 'You don't pray for God to change what is because he has a plan. You pray for God to give you the strength to make it through.' So, that is what I do. I pray for God to provide Grams and me with the strength we need to make it through whatever he has planned.

# 21

## REID

I was up early as usual to start my day. I need to run out to one of the job sites to make sure the guys posted all the proper permits on the board outside the office trailer. The place is shut down for the day, and Nikolai received a heads-up yesterday an inspector may drop by to make sure our building permits were up to date. The city has a job to do, too, looking for violations, but I run a tight crew, which means they won't find shit.

It feels fuckin' great to be back in the thick of things—back to working full-time. I'm working on my second cup of coffee when Mila comes sauntering into the kitchen wearing nothing but one of my shirts and her long, thick, black hair piled on top of her head. As she reaches into the cabinet above the coffee maker to grab a mug, her shirt rises, rewarding me a brief glimpse of her bare ass.

"Fuck, Kitten, you're killin' me," I groan. Standing, I grab my cut from the back of the chair and slip it on.

"What?" She feigns innocence and looks over her left shoulder, locking her smoldering eyes with mine.

She knows I'm heading out to take care of work-related shit

before we load up and head to Logan's lake house. Today is Sofia's birthday, and she insisted on having a pool party. Logan has the pool and the space to invite the whole crew out for a huge celebration. I'm hoping some girl time and fun in the sun will help Mila put aside her worries for a while. She has been stressed out due to the fact her Grams has fallen ill and is having a hard time getting better. A little downtime might be just what Mila needs, even if it's only for the day.

"You sure you have to go?" Mila asks, sipping her coffee as she walks toward me. She's making it damn hard to leave now when all I can think about is her sweet pussy squeezing my cock. She sits her mug on the table. Taking the opportunity, I reach for her and pull her into me. Cupping her face in my hands, I place my lips on hers. Melting into my embrace, Mila deepens our kiss while running her hands up my chest. If we keep this up, I won't leave. Reluctantly, I break our kiss and press my forehead to hers, "You're making me want to stay," I admit. Biting her bottom lip, she smiles as her mouth hovers over mine. "I love you."

"I love you too, Kitten," I respond.

Taking a step back, I plant a softer kiss on her lips. "I've got to run. I'll be back in no less than an hour." I clear my throat and try to suppress my raging hard-on with the palm of my hand.

"Be careful. I'll have Ava and myself ready to go when you get here," she says, grabbing her coffee from the table and making her way toward the hallway, putting an extra sway in her hips.

Stepping outside, I mount my bike and take in the warmth of the summer sun beating down on my face. I don't know how I got so damn lucky. Having Mila in my life has given me something I never knew I was missing before. A sense of peace—of completion.

After wrapping shit up at the job site, I make it back home to find an eager Ava bouncing around the living room decked out in her bathing suit, sunglasses, and blown up floaties stuck on each arm.

"Yay! We get to go to a pool party now!" she exclaims, throwing her hands up with excitement. Mila is over by the kitchen table packing the rest of their pool gear. I stop and take her in. She's dressed in a pair of blue jean shorts that show off her long toned legs and a cropped, black Rolling Stones t-shirt covering up the black bikini I know she's wearing underneath. She turns and catches me taking her in and smiles. Her bright eyes and beautiful smile make me feel as if the earth at my feet has crumbled beneath me. There is no other way to describe the depth of what my heart feels for her. The love I have surrendered to is transcending.

"You ready?" she asks in a breathy tone bringing my feet back down to the ground.

"Yeah, babe. I'll grab everything. You grab Ava," I tell her. Knowing she packed me some trunks in case I decide to get in the water. I grab the bags she packed and the presents we purchased in my hands, and we ride the elevator to the first floor. Once outside, I load everything into the trunk of her car, her new car.

Last week I took her to the dealership downtown and told her to pick out what she wanted. Of course, she tried to give me lip more than one time, but I wasn't budging on this. She needed a reliable car, and her old rust bucket was on its last leg. Giving in, she ended up picking out a black Range Rover Sport.

I would never have thought I'd be driving around town in a family car. The guys have been quick to give me shit over the fact as well, and I wouldn't have it any other way. Although, nothing can and never will replace my bike and the freedom I get on the open road, or the memories I get to soak up and relive when driving my brother's truck.

After making a quick stop at the store to pick Ava up some sunscreen, we arrive at Logan's. Knowing everyone is near the pool and lake area, we make our way around back. Music is playing, and kids are already in the pool having fun.

"Hey, brother. Glad you made it. Take a load off and come have a beer with the rest of us!" Logan calls from the other end of the yard just near the water's edge, where he's sitting in a lawn chair along with Quinn and Gabriel.

"I got all this," Mila states, "go have a good time with your brothers."

Setting the bags down on the patio table to my left, I hook my arm around her waist/ "Go look for the girls. You know where to find me," then I kiss her.

I watch her walk into the house with Ava before turning and making my way over toward the guys. I grab one of the empty chairs and plant my ass in it. When I lean back, Gabriel reaches into the cooler sitting beside him and tosses me a cold beer. Cracking it open, I chug half the bottle. The cold crisp taste goes down smooth. Looking out at the reflective lake, I relax in my seat. I think I needed a day off just as much as Mila did. Life has thrown some damn wrenches into the works over the past few months. Many of us have come a long fuckin' way from where we once were. I take another pull from my bottle and enjoy the stillness of the moment. Catching a glimpse of blue out the corner of my eye, I turn my head to see Alba walk up with baby Gabe on her hip.

"What the fuck is that?" Gabriel's voice booms, causing the rest of us to look on confused as to why he sounds so pissed off.

"What are you talking about?" Alba starts to check every square inch of the baby's exposed skin.

"That." Gabriel points his finger at her and gestures up and down to what she's wearing.

"It's called a bikini." Alba cocks her head to the side and huffs.

"Cover-up. You got too much tit showing," he growls at her.

Rolling her eyes, she hands their son over to him. "He wants his Papi. Could you entertain him while I take a dip in the pool?"

she asks him, then softly kisses the baby's cheek and gives a brooding Gabriel one too, before heading over to the pool.

"Damn, who knew a pregnant woman could be so sexy," Quinn remarks, knowing he's poking the bear.

Ignoring him, Gabriel tucks his son into his side and warmly smiles as he looks down at his boy, who's making vroom vroom noises while playing with the toy motorcycle in his chubby little hands. Out of all my brothers, most people would look at him and never in a million years say he's a dad. But if I'm honest, watching Gabriel with his son and seeing how natural he is with the whole role, I would say it suits him more than any other title he has in life. I want that. I want that with Mila. I want to have a large family. Have as many kids as she's willing to give me.

"How's the baby-making going, Logan?" Quinn asks as he pops the top off a bottle of beer. Logan told me awhile back that he and Bella have been trying with no luck. Quinn, on the other hand, either knows because he and Bella are close friends, or it may be due to the fact the little fucker seems to always know what's going on with everyone. He's more observant than most people give him credit for.

"The same, but I'm havin' fun trying brother, that's for sure." He grins, lifting a beer from the cooler.

"Holy shit. Look at the tats on Emerson," Quinn says, droolin'. I'll be damned. Who would have thought Emerson had all that ink under her scrubs. "Fellas, I don't know about you, but three fine as hell women just walked out that house wearing next to nothin', and one of them has my name all over her sweet ass." Quinn stands. The rest of us eye them over our shoulders. There standing by the pool in their tiny bikinis talking to Alba, who's laid back sunbathing, are Bella, Mila, and Emerson.

"She won't even give you the time of day," I tell him.

"Oh, she's mine. She just doesn't know it yet," Quinn says with certainty.

My eyes zone in on Mila. I watch her laugh with the rest of the women. *Fuck.* It's official. My favorite color on her besides those gorgeous honey colored eyes is black. Standing at the same time as Logan, his eyes trained on Bella and her tiny green bikini, we walk toward the four of them.

Stepping up to the women, I come up behind Mila and kiss her neck. "You enjoying yourself?"

"I am," she tells me.

Running my fingers down her arm, I let my warm breath dance across her ear as I whisper, "You wear this for me?"

I watch her lip turn up with a mischievous grin. "Maybe," she tells me.

I pull her into me, pressing my hard length against her ass.

"You're fuckin' perfect, Mila Vaughn," I kiss her neck again, causing her skin to break out in goosebumps.

"Come on, sunshine," Quinn begs as he towers over Emerson, who has walked off. I've never, not in all the time I've known Quinn, seen a woman turn him down. Whatever he gives them, they always come back for more. Not with Emerson, and it's thrown him for a loop. I don't know what to think about this one. Either he is in it for the thrill of the chase, or he has caught what the rest of us have. We all watch happens next. Emerson stops, turns and faces him, appearing to listen to what he might have to say. He attempts to lean down and whisper something in her ear, but as soon as he does, she places the palms of her hands on his chest then gives him a firm shove. Catching him entirely off guard, he falls backward into the pool, water spraying those of us close enough.

"Dumbass," Gabriel mumbles, placing Gabe on Alba's lap.

"What did I miss?" Nikolai asks, walking around the corner of the house with his hands full of grocery bags. Sam and Leah are right behind him carrying a cake box. I look around. I think the whole family has finally shown up. Except for Prez. I don't see him anywhere. It's not like him to not show up to things like this. "Where's Prez?" I ask no one in particular.

"He called earlier this morning. He said he'd be late, but he'd be here. Something is going on with him. I'm not sure what. You know he's tight-lipped about personal shit. He doesn't share with no one," Logan explains, gaining all our attention. I've noticed Jake has been a little edgier than usual this past week. I hope everything's alright. As Logan said, Jake doesn't share anything outside of club business with any one.

I've yet to let go of Mila, just as Logan has a tight hold of Bella, and Gabriel has sat his large-ass frame down on the lounge chair Alba was on and has her on his lap, with the baby on hers.

Nikolai walks inside for a few minutes then walks back out with a timid Leah following behind him, holding a platter of burgers to cook on the grill. She's always as quiet as a mouse. She hardly says a word to anyone, preferring to keep to herself, but I've noticed Nikolai has taken an interest in her. I'm not sure if it's sexually though. He's very gentle in the way he talks and approaches her.

Hearing giggles and splashing, I look off to the side in the grassy area next to the pool and watch Ava playing in the little blow-up kiddie pool set up for the smaller kids. It's a good thing too because, between Sofia, her friends from school, and some of the member's kids, a good dozen teenagers are hanging out in the ground pool.

"Looks like Sam has taken a liking to Sofia." Nikolai gestures as he points the spatula in his hand toward the other side of the pool.

We take notice of Sam standing with Sofia. The two of them talking and smiling at one another when Sam reaches up and pushes her fallen hair from her face.

"Oh, I wouldn't worry about Sam, guys. He's not interested in Sofia," Alba says, brushing it off and giving her attention back to the squirming baby in her arms. It looks like nothin' to me, and I'm sure my brothers feel the same.

"What the hell do you mean nothin' to worry about? He has a dick, and he's lookin' at her as if he wants her for dessert." Logan lets go of Bella and clenches his fists at his side. Oh, hell. This is not going to end well if we don't get Sam away from Sofia.

"Sam is gay," Leah softly says from beside Nikolai.

"Leah," both Alba and Bella chastise.

"Like hell, he is. That boy is not gay," I add.

Nikolai softly talks to Leah. Low enough, no one else can hear, but whatever he says helps her to relax. "I can assure you, ladies; you are wrong," he turns and addresses us all.

Well, it doesn't matter because while we were over here discussing Sam's sexual orientation, Quinn took it upon himself to break up the little moment the two were having and currently is having a talk with Sam.

"Where is the birthday girl?" Prez's voice booms over the sound of music and kids as he strides toward everyone.

Sofia runs over and stands on her tiptoes and hugs his neck, and he hands her a small wrapped box.

"Thank you, Jake. Where's Grace?" she asks, looking around.

"Couldn't make it, sweetheart," he looks down at her and gives a forced smile. "Open it," he tells her.

Tearing the paper off, she pulls the top off the small box in her hand. "Oh, my goodness! It's so pretty." Lifting the gift from the box, she shows off a delicate, gold chain with a small gold cross dangling at the end. Handing it to Jake, she waits for him to put in on her. Like with the rest of us, Jake is the father figure in our lives, and with Sofia, it's been no different. Unfortunately for her, she now also has several brothers too.

An hour later, everyone gathers to find a seat at one of the many fold-out tables that have been set up in a row. A tired, water-logged Ava sits between Mila and me, chewing on the cheeseburger in her hands. I honestly can't remember the last time I felt this happy and content.

"You have an amazing family, Reid," Mila says as she takes in all the faces at the table.

"*We* have an amazing family, babe," I tell her.

## 22

### MILA

A few days after Sofia's birthday party, I got the call that Grams had taken a turn for the worse, and they transported her to the hospital. Though the doctors had been telling me to prepare for this exact outcome, it still doesn't seem real. And hearing the doctor in charge of Grams' care at the hospital reminded me of her DNR also made the situation even more real. I've known for a few years now.

When we first received the news of her Alzheimer's diagnosis, Grams informed me of her decision to have a DNR. I tried arguing with her about it. I wanted her to change her mind, but she had decided, and it was final. She didn't want to spend any of her remaining life, if something were to happen, being kept alive by machines. In the end, I owed it to her to respect her choice; it's her life. That and she wanted the decision to be hers while she was still in the right frame of mind to choose for herself. When Grams explained it to me that way, I understood. I wouldn't want someone I loved to have the burden of making that choice for me. And she was adamant that she wouldn't place me in the position of deciding. Not only was my grandmother looking out for her wishes, but she was also looking out for me.

My grandmother is 87 years old. The elderly have a much more difficult time fighting any illness. What started as a simple cold, quickly turned into pneumonia. The doctors are treating her with antibiotics and trying to make her as comfortable as possible. I'm trying to remain hopeful. But with each day that passes and her showing no apparent signs of improvement, I lose a little more hope.

Through all this, Reid has been my rock. I don't know what I would do without him by my side. For the past few days, when he gets off work, he picks Ava up from either Alba's or the garage if it's Bella's day with her. He then takes her home, cooks her dinner, and makes sure she has her bath. He does all of that, so after I get off work, I can go straight to the hospital and sit with Grams until 9:00 pm when visiting hours are over.

By the time I make it home every night, I'm exhausted. On top of that, I feel guilty because Ava is already asleep by the time I get home. The only time I see my daughter is in the mornings over breakfast. My sweet girl hasn't complained once. I explained to her that great grandma is sick, and momma needs to be with her as much as possible. I don't think people give children enough credit on how much understanding they have because my little girl understands. She even makes Grams a new picture every day for me to take to her when I visit.

Finishing up with my last patient of the day, I look down at my watch and see it's 6:00 pm and time for me to clock out. Making my way to the nurse's station, I walk behind the counter and grab my things.

"See you tomorrow, Mila," Vanessa, a fellow nurse, says.

"Goodnight, Vanessa," I return, slinging my purse over my shoulder. Stepping outside, I pause for a moment and take in a deep breath of the fresh air.

The sun is setting just behind the mountains lighting the sky with red and orange mixed with a few grey clouds. The sunsets are my favorite thing about Montana. Growing up, Grams and I would eat dinner outside on the porch in the summer so that we could watch the sunset. A tradition we carried on up until she moved into the nursing home. Looking at the sky now, I make a vow to bring the tradition back with my daughter, and I smile.

Walking down the hall of the hospital toward my grandmother's room, I catch Dr. Hayes just as he's exiting. "Good evening, Dr. Hayes, how is she doing today?"

"Hey there, Ms. Vaughn," he says, holding my grandmother's chart down by his side. "I'm sorry to say, but Mrs. Scott's condition is the same. I started her on a new antibiotic this afternoon, so let's give it twenty-four hours to see how she responds. She has been resting comfortably all day, and we are doing all we can to get her well," Dr. Hayes explains.

"Okay, this new medicine... do you think it will work?"

Dr. Hayes shakes his head, "It's hard to say. As you know, everyone responds differently to medications, Ms. Vaughn. The best we can do is give it time to work, and we'll see how she is in the morning."

Letting out a sigh of frustration, I nod and thank the doctor before making my way into my Grams' room. The first thing I notice is the massive arrangement of sunflowers. I know I have Bella to thank for the flowers. I remember telling her they were Grams' favorite. Plucking the card from the vase, I see that I'm right; they're from Bella. My heart swells with how much my friends care.

I couldn't ask for better people. They are my family. I'm beginning to see what he means by that. They may not be blood, but they've treated me better than my own family aside from Grams. I am beyond blessed to be a part of such a big family. They have taught me that sometimes the family you choose is better than the one you are born into, and in my case, it rings true. The Kings have shown my daughter and me more love and compassion in just a few short months than my parents did in all my twenty-five years of life.

With my parents, I was only there to serve their purpose. Go to the best schools. Become a lawyer just like them and then marry a man of their choosing. And because I chose to do something they did not agree with, I no longer had any worth in their eyes. Therefore, I was disposable. Now the club is a whole different story. They didn't care who I was or where I came from. I belong to Reid, and that is all the club cares about. From that point on, Ava and I have been family. No questions asked and no hidden agenda.

The club may not operate on the right side of the law at times, and Reid has never given any details to what sorts of things The Kings are involved with, and frankly, I don't want to know. It's none of my business. In my eyes, they are all good men, regardless of their less than legal activities. Then you have people like Richard and Susan Vaughn who, on the outside and on paper, look like upstanding citizens, but underneath the façade, they are the worst of the worst. People like my parents are real criminals. They hide behind a mask. I like how the club doesn't hide who they are. What you see is what you get.

When first meeting the guys, I'll admit I was nervous. You hear all the rumors around town, and people fill your head with crazy stories about how mean and dangerous they are. I learned quickly these men are only mean and nasty to anyone who dares to fuck with their family. And after getting to know them, I wasn't in the least bit shocked to find out how much they give back to their community. The club is involved in several charities. The problem with a lot of people in this town is they refuse to look past their cuts. What makes these men even more extraordinary is that they don't give a shit what people think.

Dragging my tired behind out of my car, I'm met with Reid,

who is standing in the doorway of his house, greeting me with a warm smile.

"Kitten," he murmurs into my ear when I get close enough for him to pull me in for a hug, and I close my eyes breathing his scent. The woodsy-pine scent of his soap instantly relaxes me. "Come on, babe. You look beat, how about you go take a shower, and then I'll feed you."

Wrapping my arms around his middle, I sigh into his chest. "How did I get so lucky? You're too good to me, Reid Carter."

"I'm the lucky one, Mila. I don't know what a bastard like me did to deserve a woman like you Kitten, but I plan on spending every day proving I'm worthy of keeping you. Starting with feeding you dinner." Kissing my lips and then my nose, Reid ushers me toward the bedroom. "Go on, Kitten. Go shower."

Obeying his orders, I make my way down the hall and stop by Ava's room to peek in on her and see she is fast asleep. After a quick kiss on her head, I walk out of her bedroom, making sure to leave her door cracked open before heading to Reid's room for a shower.

I don't know how long I stand under the spray of the hot water. It must have been too long because the next thing I hear is Reid coming into the bathroom and listening to him open the shower door. No words are spoken as he leans over and turns the water off. He grabs the towel off the rack and wraps it around my body before lifting me out. Once I'm placed back on my feet, Reid proceeds to unwrap the towel and dry me off. When he finishes his task, he tosses the towel to the floor before picking me up and carrying me out of the bathroom and gently lays me down on his bed. His cool sheets feel good on my hot skin. Without taking his eyes off me, I watch him undress. I swallow up the sight of Reid, from his sculpted chest and six-pack abs, down to his thick, swollen cock; it causes the need between my thighs to intensify and when he leans his body over mine, and my legs open for him.

"I don't want you to do anything but lay here and let me take care of you, Kitten," he says just before taking my nipple into his mouth. Oh hell, who am I to argue with that? Reid lazily takes his time feasting on my breast, teasing me to the point I think I could come from that alone. And no matter how bad my need to come is, I don't say a word. Instead, I allow him to set the pace. I'm in no rush tonight. I'm going to lay here and let my man take his time while I enjoy every ounce of pleasure he brings me.

With every touch, every tease, he brings me closer to the edge. Finally, he enters me. His broad tip is guiding its way in, and my pussy clenches down on his thick cock so hard it causes him to growl. The blistering heat of our bodies and the slow controlled rhythm of his cock rocking in and out of me causes my body to shiver close to the peak of orgasm. Reid's teeth bite down on the side of my neck in the grip of possession before he runs his tongue along his mark soothing the sting.

Taking my wrists and pinning them over my head, a fierce rumble rips through him as he begins fucking me harder, yet keeping his touch gentle. The combination of the two driving me wild. His moans start to get lost in mine, and the tendons in his neck strain with every thrust. I'm hypnotized by the rippling of his broad shoulders and chiseled arms as he holds himself above me. When I feel his cock swell, it triggers my orgasm, and I come, causing my vision to blacken with its intensity. When my pussy clamps down on Reid's cock, he can no longer hold off his impending orgasm. With two final thrusts, he plants himself deep inside me, filling me.

I startle awake sometime later with the shrill ringing of my cell phone. Sitting up in bed, I look at the clock on the bedside table that reads 2:00 am. *Who the hell is calling me at this time of the morning?* Picking up my phone from the table, my body stills, and my heart stops. I recognize the number on the screen. It's the hospital. There is only one reason the hospital would be calling me at 2:00 am. I feel the bed move beside me.

"Babe, who is it?" Reid asks.

Ignoring his question, I answer my phone. "Hello?"

"Ms. Vaughn, it's Doctor Hayes. I'm sorry to be calling you at this hour, but..." his words get cut off when I speak. "She's gone, isn't she?" I ask, my voice shaky. I know I'm right. I feel it deep in my bones; with everything I am, I feel it. Grams is gone. "Yes, Ms. Vaughn. I'm sorry."

Those are the last words I hear Dr. Hayes say before I lose my grip on the phone, and it falls to the floor. A second later, I let out a strangled cry before Reid's strong arms engulf me. We don't speak, he knows what I need without asking and holds me. For hours he embraces me and lets me cry until my body finally gives out, and I can no longer weep. Sitting in the middle of his bed, Reid holds me as I stare blankly out the bedroom window watching as the sun rises over the mountain, and the warm sun shines through casting a blanket of heat over our fused bodies. Lost in the stillness of the moment, I think back to what Grams used to always say, *You don't pray for God to change what is because he has a plan. You pray for God to give you the strength to make it through.*

---

THE PAST FOUR days have gone by in a blur. Reid and the club once again stepped up and were quick to help in any way they could. It meant the world to me he was willing to stick with me through all the bumps in the/fffqa road. There are few men like him out in the world. Most people might haul ass; not Reid. I feel like his life has been chaos ever since I stepped foot into his house for the first time. At one point, I even apologized. He quickly shot down my apology and informed me he would tan my ass if he ever heard me say shit like that again.

Grams' funeral was quick. She already had arrangements in place, and everything paid for. She thought of everything. The whole club showed up along with her longtime nurse from the nursing home. I even caught a glimpse of River in the back of the crowd. Reid, of course, was by my side holding my hand while Ava was tucked in his arm as we lay my grandmother to rest alongside my grandfather. I stood in front of the crowd and said a few words about who Charlotte Scott was and recanted a couple of my favorite memories of her. In the end, I did as Grams requested. I kept it short and sweet.

The cemetery cleared, everyone heading to Logan and Bella's house because she and Lisa insisted on handling the wake. I stayed behind to watch as they lowered my grandmother; the slow descent into the earth making her death more final. Tearing my eyes away from the hole in the ground, I lift my face toward the sky; I see the sun setting. It dawns on me why my grandmother chose this time of day for her funeral. With the mountains lit up in purple, and the sky bathed in pinkish-orange hues, I root myself in a moment of clarity. My Grams is still with me. This request was not for her. It was for me.

## 23

# REID

It's hard. Moving on after losing someone you love, losing a person who helped you become who you are today. Not having their physical presence by your side causes instability because an essential piece of your structure is gone. That's how I felt when I lost not only Noah but my old man as well. I imagine that's how Mila is feeling. Her grams was her lifeline for so long. The only love she felt her entire life until our paths crossed. The pain of loss never goes away. I know. I still feel the sting of sorrow every day, but you learn to live with it.

Inner strength.

We all have it.

For some, it takes awhile to find, but it's there.

Watching her now as she stands in front of the bathroom mirror, dressed in her standard work scrubs preparing to start a new day, I see that strength in her. I can sit here on the edge of my bed and claim to be the stronger sex, but that would be a lie. The woman standing before me has strength beyond any man. Bending down, I tie the laces on my work boots before standing and walking up behind her. "Hey, beautiful. I gotta get goin'. I'll be on the site working with the crew today. You need something, you call." I kiss the top of her head. After painting her lips with her favorite red lipstick, she spins to face me. I run my fingers through her soft hair causing her eyes to close momentarily.

"I was thinking," she sighs, reopening her eyes.

"About what, Kitten?"

While I get lost in the gold specks of her eyes, she tells me, "I'm ready."

I smile when she smiles. "And what are you ready for?" I ask, planting a kiss on her temple.

"To move forward. I don't need the trial period, Reid. I know what I want. I want to stay here. Permanently."

I let her words sink in. I know what she feels for me, but Mila has been apprehensive about making a full commitment. She was still somewhat guarded, and she had every right to be. Trusting someone with your heart isn't easy. With my mouth hovering over hers, I admit with a grin, "Wasn't plannin' on letting you go, babe," and then I kiss her.

---

I'M NOT that boss who does nothing but sit behind a desk pushing papers. I'm the one working side by side with my men. I'm a firm believer in leading by example to show them what I expect from my employees.

It's hot as fuck by Montana's standards today, so the rest of the crew and I are taking a water break. As I'm walking over to the office trailer, a black car pulls up. I pull a bandana from my back pocket to wipe the sweat from my brow as I watch River step out of his car.

"Reid, you got a minute?" he asks, shaking my hand.

"Got about ten minutes I can spare," I inform him.

"I can't get in touch with Mila. I need to finalize her grandmother's will with her."

She told me the other day she was dodging his calls because she wasn't ready to deal with any of it just yet. I don't blame her, and I wasn't about to push the issue. When she was ready, she would say something. By her words this morning, I think now would be a good time to take care of it. "How about I give her a call. See if I can get her to come by later today," I tell him.

River nods, "Sounds like a plan. I'm sorry to have bothered you at work. I'll be in my office until 5:00 pm today."

I down the rest of the bottled water I was holding in my hand, "Alright," I answer.

Once he gets back in his car and pulls away, I dig my phone out of my back pocket and call Mila.

She answers on the third ring. "Hey, is everything okay?"

"Yeah, babe, everything is good. Listen, you feeling up to going by River's today? You've got to take care of your Grams' will," I ask her. The line is silent. I know she's contemplating.

Hearing her exhale, she answers, "Okay. It's time I take care of it. Will you go with me? I think I can get off an hour early today if I ask now."

"Yeah, Kitten. You need me. You got me," I tell her.

"I'll meet you at his office...and Reid?" she says, pausing, "I love you."

"Love you too, beautiful. I'll see you later," I tell her before we end our call.

A few hours later, I'm pulling up in front of River's office building to find Mila sitting in her car waiting. Hearing the rumble of my bike, she gets out and slings her bag over her shoulder.

"Hey," she walks up to the side of my bike after I've backed in beside her car.

Hangin' my helmet on my handlebar, I pull her into my lap while I'm still sitting. "Hey, babe. Been waiting long?"

"Maybe ten minutes. Not long," she tells me and runs her fingers through my hair before tracing the tattoo on the side of my head.

"You ready?" I ask her.

"Ready," she responds, kissing me before she stands.

Getting off my bike, I grab her hand in mine, and we walk inside. We don't have to wait because River is standing outside his office door and ushers us in. Taking the two seats on the other side of his desk, we sit while he walks over to a large file cabinet and pulls out a sealed manila folder.

"Thanks for stopping by, Mila. How are you holding up? I haven't seen you since the funeral," River inquires, sitting down.

He hands the envelope over to Mila, and she answers him, "Doing better, River. Thank you for asking."

"Everything's there," he tells her as she pulls the papers out and starts to flip through them. "She left you everything. The house, which was always in her and your grandfather's name. And money. You'll have to sign some papers before I can transfer everything to your name. That should only take a couple of weeks before everything gets finalized," he informs her.

Quietly she sits and takes her time reading everything. When Mila finishes looking it over, she hands them to me.

"How long did Grams know about the money?" Mila asks River.

"I'm not sure. Mrs. Scott, your grandmother, brought me legal papers and other documents your grandfather left behind that she found buried in her closet. That's when I discovered the money and told her about it. But that was also after she came in to draw up her will shortly after being diagnosed with Alzheimers," he tells her.

"So, it's a good possibility she merely forgot. That she didn't even remember anything about the money?" Mila mumbles.

It makes sense. I don't think her grandmother would have kept something like that from her. She knew how hard Mila worked to make ends meet and the sacrifices she made through life. If she had remembered, she would have made sure Mila knew and helped her financially.

"You ready to sign papers today, babe? Or do you wanna wait?" I ask her.

Sitting straighter, I see the strength I admire in her shine through, "I'm ready."

She signs everything and walks out of the office thirty minutes later, and we head straight to Logan and Bella's house to pick up Ava. Since Bella kept Ava all day, it makes the rest of the evening grind less hectic on Mila when Bella offers to feed us dinner too. I picked up the slack for awhile just after her Grams passed because let's face it, Mila has been through one thing after the other for awhile now. Eventually, everything finally caught up with her. So, I stepped up my game and put my nonexistent domestic skills to use. It wasn't always smooth running. I'm still learning all the curves that come along with taking care of a four-year-old. I don't know how Mila has done it by herself for so long.

Logan and I are sitting outside on the deck in their backyard while we watch Ava play with a puppy. Logan told me he was thinking of surprising Bella with a dog the other day when I swung by the clubhouse to have a few beers after work with the guys. "You realize in a few months you'll have piles of shit the size of boulders in your backyard, right?" I lean back in my chair.

"It's what she wanted, brother," he states.

We both stare on as Ava plays tug of war with a Great Dane puppy.

"That dog will be bigger than Bella is," I laugh.

"She'll make a good watchdog. Who's gonna mess with her if she has that walking beside her?" Logan pleads his case.

Mila and Bella walk out the sliding glass doors bringing Logan and I a glass of iced tea. Snagging her by the waist, I pull Mila onto my lap, and Logan does the same with Bella.

"Logan, there are chairs that I can sit in," she teases.

"You'll sit your ass right here where I want it. Don't sass me, woman; I just bought you a really expensive guard dog." He pulls her in tighter making her feet dangle off the ground.

She rolls her eyes. "I already have you," she says, then kisses him.

Ava slowly walks up to her momma while trying to carry the pup in her arms. "Momma, I want a doggie," she giggles when the puppy lifts its head and laps at her face with its tongue.

I chuckle, and it causes Mila to turn around, giving me a stern 'she doesn't need a dog' look. Shit, I'd give either one of them whatever they want. If her momma were to say yes, I would go out and get a puppy tomorrow if it made them happy.

"I'm sure you can come to play with this one anytime you want, sweetie," Mila tells her then looks to Bella to help her out.

"You can come to play with her anytime you want," Bella smiles and confirms.

"Yay!" Ava giggles and continues toward the grass to play.

We sit a while enjoying the cool evening breeze. The sun is starting to set, casting an orange glow across the tops of the trees as the lightning bugs begin to randomly flicker on and off while they hover over the water's surface.

"I want to sell Grams' house," Mila says, softly, breaking the silence.

"Babe, you sure?" I ask her, knowing it means a great deal to her and holds so many memories. I can't have her give that up because I want her to live with me.

"What if I moved into the house with you?" I offer.

She is quick with her answers and firmly says, "No. I want to stay where we are. I'm happy there. Ava is happy there. No. I'm selling the house. The sooner, the better," she states. Shifting her body, she faces me. "Will you help me pack? I have tomorrow off."

"Yeah, babe." I take her face in my hands and kiss her.

Relaxing for the first time today, she sinks back into me. We end up staying until the sun has set before saying our goodbyes and head home.

---

THE NEXT DAY with Ava in tow, we turn onto the street to Mila's house and roll up to see all my brothers waitin' in the driveway with a moving truck. I imagine Logan called in reinforcements after last night's conversation. It's what family does for one another. You shouldn't have to ask someone to be there for you. They should already be there willing to help. Mila is still getting used to the fact that she has become a part of the family. It still overwhelms her. The same as it did when everyone was there to show support and respect when Grams passed away. Day in and day out, someone was there. Whether they cooked her food or took care of Ava or merely checked on her, they were there. "You good with them helpin' out, Kitten?" I ask her to be sure.

She swipes a lone tear from her cheek as we come to a stop, and I turn off the engine.

"More than good," she whispers.

She unbuckles herself and her daughter, then her and the rest of the women go inside to get things started. I walk up to my brothers, who are gathered on the front lawn talking. Since we're just the muscle for the day, we hang back and let the ladies do what they need to do.

"Hey, brothers," I greet them.

"Heard you could use the help," Prez speaks up. "She really sellin' the place? It's a nice, quiet neighborhood."

It is a good neighborhood. Quiet because most of the residents are on the older side, and most of the properties around here are well maintained. I'm still kind of shocked she was willing to let go of it so fast. I decided not to bring the issue up to her again after we got home last night. It's her choice. I only hope she and her daughter can be happy in the long run living in town. I have a backyard, but it's much smaller than this one. Not what I would think someone would want to raise a kid in if they had another option like this home. It's on the older side. Maybe built in the early mid-seventies. A ranch-style house, but it seems to be more family oriented than what I have to offer. "Not sure that's what she wants, but she is selling it. She's set on it," I confirm.

We stand around and shoot the shit, for I don't know how long. Mostly we throw around the idea of doing a charity run sometime soon. We do a few every year. The one comin' up helps fund a charity that supports our veterans.

"We have some stuff ready to get loaded in here," Bella announces while stepping out onto the porch.

While my brothers start hauling boxes marked for my place—strike that—our home, I search the house for Mila and find her in her Grams' room. She's sitting on the floor surrounded by boxes that have been taped up and has a photo in her hand. "Hey, babe. You okay?"

She cranes her head back to look up at me, "I'm good. I was looking through some old pictures and came across an old one of Grams and my grandpa back from when they started dating in high school," she says, handing me the picture. I stare at the grainy black and white photograph in my hand. It's uncanny how much she looks like her grandmother. I give the photo back to her, and she places it in a box.

"I didn't think it would be so hard packing everything away." She goes to get up, and I help her stand.

"You're allowed to change your mind about selling the house," I tell her.

"No. I still want to sell. It does me no good sitting here when another family could build their own memories in a home that held so much love."

I don't ever get tired of being amazed by her kindness. I wrap my arms around her and hold her for a moment.

Come lunchtime, we all paused long enough to eat the sandwiches Lisa had fixed for everyone. By late afternoon the women have everything wrapped and boxed. Looking more mentally exhausted than physically, I told Mila to head home for the day with Ava, and I'd catch a ride back once we finished.

By the time I get home, it's late. Jake dropped me off, and I dragged my tired ass inside lookin' for nothin' but a hot shower and the comfort of my woman by my side. Quietly, I make my way to the kitchen and grab a slice of room temperature pizza from the box sitting on the counter and eat it as I walk down the hallway. I stop long enough to peek in on Ava, who is sound asleep holding her teddy. When I get to our bedroom, Mila is sleeping in the bed with one bare leg stuck out from under the covers. Taking the last bite of my food, I strip from my clothes, walk into the bathroom and turn the shower on.

I sit under the spray of hot water until it starts to run cold. Once I've dried off and taken care of all my other nightly shit, I head to bed. I feel Mila's body shift as I ease myself under the covers. Lying on my back, I pull her close.

Mila isn't much of a spooner. She prefers to drape her body over mine. Sometimes to the point of sleeping on top of me. As soon as her head is tucked under my chin and her body melts into mine, I relax, letting the feel of her warm, wispy breath across my skin lull me to sleep.

## 24

## MILA

Last night I brought up the subject of paying Reid back for my new car. He argued it wasn't going to happen. He said my car was a piece of shit death trap, and it was his job to take care of Ava and me, to make sure we were safe. "My car may have been a piece of shit, but I paid for it myself, and it has gotten me where I need to go," I had fumed. Reid's face had softened at my words. He knows I struggled at times, and I did the best I could for being a single mother. I didn't have much, but Ava has never wanted for anything, even if that meant I had to drive a shitty car.

Later that day, I told him I hadn't meant to get so worked up. I knew he didn't mean for his words to come across the way I took them. Reid would never intentionally hurt my feelings. I had already planned on going down to the dealer to at least look at a newer used car, someday. He went on to tell me he wouldn't accept any money for it in return. When he said it, I made sure to keep my temper in check; this time, as I calmly informed him, I was perfectly capable of paying him back.

He knows I can afford it now. At least once I have access to the money Grams left me. He had already informed me when we moved in, he would be paying all the household bills. I don't have anything to spend my money on.

"I don't want to be a kept woman, Reid. I want our relationship to be fifty-fifty. I appreciate that you want to take care of me, I do. But I can still take care of myself and Ava," I stressed my point.

He had let out an exasperated sigh, telling me, "Being in a committed relationship is new for me too. I'm kind of winging things as I go. I'm tryin' not to fuck shit up, babe."

That's when I walked over to him and placed my palm on his cheek. "You're not messing anything up. We're both trying to navigate the ins and outs of this relationship together. I imagine all couples who are starting out face the same obstacles. If we keep going like we are now and talk things through with each other, we'll be fine. So long as I don't go on the defense about every little thing and you try to keep your alpha male tendencies in check, we're good," I teased.

"What's got you thinkin' so hard over there, Kitten?" Reid asks.

Lost in thought, I tear my gaze from looking out the car window, and I turn my attention toward Reid.

*Lots of things.*

We're in my car on our way to the clubhouse. Reid said all the guys, along with Bella and Alba are there, and he asked me if I want to go hang out with everyone for a bit. When we were getting ready to leave the house, we argued over who was going to drive. I insisted he take his bike because I know how much he missed riding after his accident. I have Ava, so unless she is staying with someone, I never get the opportunity to ride with him like I would love to do. Reid lives to ride; all his brothers do. I don't want to take any of that away from him.

"Wherever you and Ava are, is where I'll be." That's what he told me.

I decide to keep last night's reflections to myself and bring up a different topic altogether. "I was thinking about the charity event the hospital is having, and how I've decided to give this year's speech."

"Really? That's great, babe. I'm proud of you," Reid says, reaching across the center console to hold my hand.

"Yeah, Grams would have wanted me to do it. And even though I'm terrified to stand up in front of all those people to deliver the speech, I feel it's something I need to do. The cause is too important for me to turn down the opportunity to tell my story and bring more awareness to the disease."

Bringing my hand up to his mouth, he kisses it, "You're an amazing woman, Mila Vaughn."

I break our connection when I hear my phone ringing from somewhere in my purse. Reid snickers from the driver's seat when the phone stops ringing because I didn't find it in time.

"Shut up," I giggle. I know my purse is a never-ending abyss. Reid is always joking about how I have everything but the kitchen sink in there. I argue back saying I need all my stuff until I pull out not one, not two, but three hairbrushes. And don't ask me why I just pulled out a potato peeler. Seeing me holding the peeler in my hand, Reid's head rears back, letting out a bark of laughter.

"It's not the kitchen sink, but it's pretty damn close, Kitten," he jokes, and I narrow my eyes at him.

A second later, I find my phone at the bottom of my purse. Seeing I have a new voice message I tap the screen and listen. Once I've finished listening, I toss my cell back into my bag. "That was the realtor," I divulge.

"What did the lady have to say?" Reid inquires.

"Grams' house sold."

"How do you feel about that?" he asks.

I shrug my shoulders, "I'm okay with it. I didn't expect it to sell so fast, considering how old it is. But I'm okay. It's bittersweet. I love that house. I have so many fond memories in that house, but selling it was the right decision. I couldn't imagine living there without Grams. It wouldn't feel right."

"I get it, babe. After my brother and Pops died, I couldn't stay in my childhood home. We had some good times in that house, but after losing them both, I couldn't bring myself to stay there. So, after living in the clubhouse for months, I decided to sell. Not long after that, I bought the firehouse," Reid shares.

I love it when he gives little pieces of his story to me. He has a hard time opening up, so I cherish every part of himself he shares with me.

When we pull up to the clubhouse, Reid steps out and automatically goes to get Ava from her car seat in the back, and doesn't stir as she rests her head on Reid's shoulder while walking inside. Gabriel is the first to greet us.

"Hey, brother. Why don't you take Ava to lay down with Gabe? He's taking a nap in Alba's old room. I have the monitor," he says, taking a baby monitor from his back pocket and showing us.

Giving Gabriel a nod, Reid turns toward me. "I'm going to put her down, why don't you go find the girls? They're probably in the kitchen with Lisa. Maybe you could offer to peel some potatoes," he smirks.

I place my hands on my hips, "You're never going to let me live that down, are you?"

"Not a fuckin' chance, Kitten," he says to my retreating back as I flip him the bird over my shoulder.

"What was that about?" Quinn pipes up.

"Nothing," Reid and I say in unison.

"Finally," Bella says when I walk into the kitchen. "Where's my sweet girl?" she inquires about Ava.

"Ava fell asleep on the way here, so Reid is putting her down for a nap with Gabe," I tell her. Speaking of baby Gabe, I see his momma Alba sitting at the table with a bowl of cereal. "How are you feeling today, Alba?"

"My back is a little achy, but other than that I feel great." She smiles.

"Well, you look great. Pregnancy agrees with you," I let her know.

I'm startled by a gruff voice from behind me.

"I agree," Gabriel says from the doorway of the kitchen, his heated gaze on Alba. "Cariño *Sweetheart,* Gabe's asleep," he tells her. With a shy smile and a blush, she abandons her meal and goes to her man, who's holding out his hand to her. Once they leave the kitchen, Bella, Lisa, and I all look at each other before we break out in laughter, because yeah, we know what's about to go down.

An hour later, we all sit down to eat. Ava and Gabe both woke up from their naps and since Gabriel and Alba were momentarily indisposed, I took it upon myself to get Gabe settled into his highchair and feed him his lunch. It's hilarious when Alba and Gabriel finally make their appearance. Gabriel has the biggest grin on his face, whereas Alba is beet red from embarrassment because we all knew what they were up to. Of course, Quinn had to go and make it worse.

"You okay, sweetheart?" he asks Alba. "You look a little flushed."

Gabriel comes to her defense. "Fuck off, Quinn."

But it's Logan who wipes Quinn's smile off his face with his comment. "Hey Quinn, still sniffin' around Emerson? Heard she still won't give you the time of day. I think you're losing your touch, brother."

Everyone bursts out laughing at Quinn's expense. It's no secret he has a thing for Emerson, only she seems to be immune to his charm.

"I'm not losing shit. I've hit a little snag is all. I'm beginning to think she may swing the other way," Quinn announces.

"Emerson is not gay," Bella replies.

Quinn eyes Bella, "How do you know?"

Bella cocks her head to the side, debating whether she wants to give Quinn her answer. The whole table has gone silent. Probably because the shy doctor is somewhat of a mystery to us all. We all know she and Bella have become good friends, and she has been to the clubhouse a few times, but other than that, no one seems to know much about her. I'm starting to suspect Bella does. After a moment, Bella speaks up.

"She has a date tonight. With a **man**," she emphasizes.

He jolts from his chair at the table, "Who the fuck with?" Quinn demands.

All eyes are ping-ponging back and forth between Bella and Quinn at this point. Lunch has suddenly turned interesting.

"Some guy her parents set her up with," Bella gives.

No sooner do her words leave her mouth, Quinn storms away from the table. Moments later, we hear his bike start up and the sound of his tires as he peels out of the driveway leaving us all speechless. Quinn is the more laid back of the men, and I've heard of his ventures. Reid has mentioned before Quinn has never been serious about a woman. Judging by his reaction we just witnessed moments ago, he seems serious about Emerson. Either that or he's butthurt over her rejection. My vote is on the latter. No man has that kind of reaction over a woman he's only interested in getting into bed. Nope, the doctor means more than that.

"Angel, what did you do?" Logan asks Bella.

"I'm trusting my gut."

By the somber look on my friend's face, I'd say what she did wasn't for Quinn, but Emerson.

---

THE NEXT AFTERNOON I'm sitting on the living room floor going through some boxes of photo albums while Reid and Ava sit on the floor next to me playing go fish. The first album I come to is

Ava's baby book. I smile. I haven't looked at these pictures in a long time.

"What you got there, babe?"

I hold the book up and show him, "Ava's baby book. You want to look at it with me?"

"Yeah, Kitten, I'd love to."

Not interested in what Reid and I are doing, Ava cuts in, "Momma, can I watch my movie?"

"Sure, sweetheart. The DVD is already in the player, all you have to do is press play. You remember what button I showed you to press?"

Nodding her head yes, she bounces down the hall to her room. Standing up from the floor, Reid sits behind me on the sofa, and peers over my shoulder. With the photo album on my lap, I flip to the first page. The first picture is of me, Grams, and Ava the day we arrived in Polson. It was Grams' idea to start the album. I had never given much thought to it. My parents didn't have family portraits, and they weren't the type to snap pictures all the time. Not like me. I have hundreds of photos of Ava on my phone. If it wasn't for my grandmother taking pictures of me all those times I stayed with her in the summer growing up; I wouldn't have anything to pass down to my daughter. With each page, I flip through Reid listens on intently as I describe in detail how old Ava was or where we were when the pictures were taken. Realizing I have never seen any pictures of his brother or dad, I tilt my head back and ask him, "Do you have any pictures of your family? I'd love to see some." I wait with bated breath for his response.

"Yeah, babe. I have a few. I'll go get them," he says before disappearing down the hall to his room. A moment later, he returns with what looks like a shoebox. I don't question why he stores them away instead of having them out on display in the house. I know why. The first couple of pictures are of his dad and his mom. His dad is sporting The Kings of Retribution cut, and a blonde-haired woman is standing next to him. I already know about his mom. Reid confided in me one night. He told me how she ran off with another man when he and his brother were little. The next picture is of a baby boy who looks to be about a year old. "Is this you?" I ask.

"No, that's my brother. This one is me," he says, handing me the next photo.

Even if he hadn't told me it was him, I would have guessed, because the young boy in the picture has beautiful green eyes. I'd know those eyes anywhere. "You and your brother don't look too much alike," I observe.

"Nah, I look like my Pops, and Noah took after our mom."

When Reid mentions his brother's name, my heart rate picks up. He's never spoken his name before. "Your brother's name is Noah?"

His only response is a nod.

Continuing to flip through picture after picture, I feel my mouth go dry.

*It can't be. Can it?*

"Do you have a recent picture of Noah from before he passed away?" I ask with a slight tremble in my voice.

Reid looks at me with furrowed brows. "Yeah, right here," he says, reaching into the box and pulling another photograph out.

With shaky hands, I take the picture from him. Closing my eyes, I take a deep breath then look at the glossy photo in my hand. The eyes staring back at me are the same eyes I have looked at for the past four years. The same eyes that burned into mine that summer five years ago.

## 25

# REID

I don't share my memories with anyone. I've kept all but one photo of my family, which is of Noah and me, and it's located in my office. I've kept the rest of them hidden in a box in the farthest part of my closet. Hiding my pain.

I thought we were enjoying the whole reminiscing thing. I thought she wanted to know more about me. But judging by the way all color has drained from Mila's face, I'm guessing she may be having second thoughts about traveling down memory lane together. Maybe it's too much too soon? "Babe, you alright?" I ask her as I place the old shoebox on the coffee table.

Her response: silence.

"Kitten," I say to grab her attention. Her hands are shaking with the photo held tightly in her grip.

"Five years ago, I was here for the summer with Grams. Every summer I spent here was exciting, but that year..." her thoughts seem to wander as she continues to look down at her lap, "As I told you before, I never went out. No parties. I didn't hang with kids my age. I usually always spent my time with Grams. Not that she never encouraged me to experience things a normal teenager would love to do. It was just...anyway, that summer, I met this guy one afternoon down at the drugstore when I was picking up Grams' medicine. At first, I was shocked he even talked to me." She finally looks up at me, with red-rimmed eyes threatening to spill tears. She is finally opening up to me now. Finally sharing more pieces of herself with me. I urge her to continue by lowering myself to the floor sitting across from her.

After sucking in a gulp of air, Mila releases it and continues. "He invited me to a small party his friends were throwing for him," her lips turn up in a small smile at her memory of that day. "I think he could tell I was going to say no, so he gently grabbed my hand and said please. For the first time, I didn't overthink anything, and I said yes. He gave me the address, and a few hours later, I showed up on the doorsteps of a stranger's home nervous and scared out of my mind as to how far out of my comfort zone I was."

It never dawned on me until now. All the times she came for the summers, I never saw her. No. I would remember seeing her kind of beauty around town. I wouldn't have forgotten anything about her. Perhaps I was so caught up in my own life I merely never noticed. I would have been prospecting at the time, so it's not surprising that I didn't. Back then my days were filled with either working with my Pops building houses or paying my dues with the club. I didn't have too much time for much else in those days.

"He was the one who met me at the door," Mila continues talking. "He walked me through the house where the party was just getting started. I didn't know anyone there. I think he sensed my hesitation and nervousness, because he continued to weave through the crowd only stopping to grab a few beers from a cooler near the back door and walk us outside." Leaning back against the couch Mila picks up her glass of wine she has sat on the coffee table and takes a sip. "We spent all night outside in the cool summer air talking about things like him going off to college and how I wasn't looking forward to going to law school. He seemed genuinely happy with life. I remember feeling so jealous of how easy life appeared to be for him." She shifts, becoming noticeably uncomfortable as she continues to share with me. "The whole time, I couldn't take my eyes off him. He was very good looking. Tall. I would say about your height." She looks at me, "blond hair and blue eyes."

I want to hear her story, hear about her past. I want to know everything there is to know about Mila Vaughn. What I'm not too keen on listening to is the attraction she had for another man. I see where the storytelling is leading up to. I already feel my body heat starting to rise with the thought of another man having touched her body the way I have. Trying to squash my jealous feelings, I reach out to grasp her hand in mine and intertwine our fingers.

"I'm not going to go into detail with you as to what happened a short time later. It was my choice. I wanted to feel alive for once, and he made that happen for me. For one night, I felt normal. I felt free," she tells me.

He was a lucky son of a bitch. No way in hell I could have let her go that summer night. The guy didn't know what he was holding, or who he was letting go. He had to have been blind to chalk one night with Mila up to a once in a lifetime experience. "Ava's father," I confirm.

Wetting her lips, she nods her head, "Yes, he's Ava's father."

"I hope you don't mind me asking, but why isn't he in her life?" I've always wondered this, but never wanted to ask because there was never a moment that felt right until now. Until she felt she could open up to me about who he was. Anyone who can walk away from their kid gets no fuckin' respect from me. You don't create a life and then abandon them. That scenario resonates too deep with me. You don't have to love the other person to take care of your responsibilities. You shouldn't have the right to fuck a kid up like that. You're giving the gift of life. You don't throw something like that away. I sound angry and bitter because I am. Being the product of a parent abandoning me, I feel very strongly about the subject. My life was damn good even though my mom decided she didn't want us anymore, but it would be a lie to say I didn't have any underlying effects from it. "Well hell, babe. I grew up in this town. I don't think you've ever mentioned his name before. Maybe I know the guy or know of him. Shit, I may have gone to school with the asshole," I express. I want to find out straight from the source why he didn't step up. I'll find the fucker one way or another.

Mila's grip on my hand tightens. A few silent minutes pass as I wait for her to speak his name.

"Reid...I...Oh my god. I hope I'm wrong, but I don't think I am. I...his name was..." she stammers as she starts to sob softly. "I found out I was pregnant at the end of the summer before I left to go back home. That night—it was supposed to be just one night. We agreed. Or he reluctantly went along with what I wanted. I couldn't risk my heart when I knew I couldn't have anything more. My parents wouldn't allow it. I tried to find him before I left. I didn't purposely keep it from him," she frantically says as she gets more worked up. I never once thought she was the type to hide something as important as that from anyone.

"Babe, take a breath. Calm down for me," I coax her. Taking a few more deep breaths, attempting to shake her nerves, she swipes her eyes with the back of her free hand.

"When I went back to the house where the party was that night," she says looking me in the eyes, "some guys I briefly met in passing were sitting on the front porch. I walked up to them, asking them where I could find him." Tears roll down her cheeks, and I try to wipe them away only for new ones to spill down the same path.

"They told me he died. He was killed in a car crash a few days after I had met him," she continues to stare at me. A feeling of eeriness washes over me. To the point, my heart starts to pound like a jackhammer. *Summertime. Blond hair. Blue eyes. Car crash.* **MY** *hometown. Five years ago. No. No, it can't be.* It's just a fucked-up coincidence. I swallow past the large lump in my throat and ask her again, "What was his name?"

With a shaky breath, she announces, "Noah."

Immediately my hand releases hers, and she rushes to say, "But I never got his last name, Reid," she says reaching for the very hand that let go of hers. I don't know how to process this news. Robotically, I get to my feet. Afraid I may say the wrong thing. Not wanting to upset her with the mess I'm feeling consumed by on the inside, I walk to the kitchen and grab my cut from the back of the chair. Slipping it on, I grab my keys from the kitchen counter and walk toward the door. With my hand on the knob, I look over my shoulder at her. She is still sitting on the floor. Every emotion she is feeling etched on her beautiful face. They are the same feelings cutting me up on the inside. "I need space. I need to clear my head for awhile." I open the door, but make sure to tell her before stepping out of it, "I love you, Kitten."

Closing the door behind me, I go down the stairs and hop on my bike, hoping the road will help clear my head.

Riding until the sun has nearly set and no closer to sorting out my shit, I decide to ride out to the clubhouse. When I get there, the guys' bikes are parked outside. With a boulder sitting on my shoulders, I pull mine alongside Quinn's before finding my way inside. I see them all sitting at one of the round tables with a bottle of Jameson seated in the middle of the table, partially drunk. I'm not a big drinker. Never have been, but considering the last few hours, I decide tonight I want it. I need to quiet the noise in my head.

"Hey, brother." Gabriel greets me.

I don't say a word. Pulling a chair out, I plant my ass in it and reach for the bottle and pour some into a shot glass. Lifting the shot glass to my lips, I down it and pour another. I repeat the process two more times before I lean back in my chair. I take in the shocked and worried looks on their faces as I glance around the table.

"What the fuck's goin' on?" Logan asks, taking a long pull from his cigarette.

*Where the fuck do I begin?*

"Noah." It's the only word I can get to leave my lips. I'm at a complete loss as to how I say it. Say it out loud.

"What about him, brother?" Logan pours himself a shot.

I hadn't even realized the day was closing in. For once, I haven't been focused on it. I've been living again. With Mila. Blowing out a breath of air, I tell them. "Noah is Ava's father."

"What? No fuckin' way, man. Stop bullshitting us," Quinn laughs.

I lean forward and place my elbows on the table and hang my head. "I wish I were. Mila and I started sharing memories. Sharing more of our pasts while sifting through photographs. She asked to see pictures from my childhood. What I have has been kept in a box. And you all know I haven't displayed any pictures for a long time. After seeing a picture of Noah, she put her past from five summers ago together with a ghost from the past she was holding in her hands," I reach for the liquor bottle again. My brothers wait for me to explain further after I down one more shot.

"She only knew his first name. He invited her to a party. You know the night his friends threw him a going away party just before we had the one for him out here?" I remind them all.

"That was one hell of a party," Quinn adds.

Everyone looked out for Noah. He wasn't just my brother; he was theirs too.

I continue, "She said before she left for New York she found out she was pregnant and went back to the only place she thought to find him." I look around the table, "his old friend's house. That's when they had to inform her he died a few weeks prior in a car crash."

*Fuck.* The more I think about it...damn.

"That's some heavy shit, brother," Gabriel rumbles.

"She comes to this revelation and pours her soul out to you, and you're sittin' here instead of holding your woman?" Quinn sits across from me and asks.

"I need time to process everything. To think," I tell him.

"What the hell is there to think about? Do you love her?" he asks me.

"Yes." I reply. There is no doubt Mila is it for me.

"Ava is a part of Noah; she is a part of you, Reid. Your flesh and blood. Let that sink in before the whiskey you've consumed fogs your brain," Gabriel states.

He's right. Holy shit, he's fuckin' right. I've got a piece of my brother asleep in bed at home. A little girl who has me wrapped around her little finger. And the more my mind is filled with the image of her sweet face, the more I see him in her. She looks just like him. Blonde hair, blue eyes, her zest for life. She is so optimistic about everything. Smart as hell. She is every bit like Noah was, with all the caring heart and sass of her momma. My mind flashes back to the dream I had weeks ago.

*"I'm not going to California, Reid. Everything is just as it should be. It's time for you to take your life back. I need you to do something for me. I'm counting on you not to let me down."*

I'm not a person who shares their feelings. Never have been. I suck it up. I keep everything bottled up inside. But I'm also fuckin' human. It takes its toll. It doesn't matter how much of a man I am or the fact I'm a biker. None of that shit matters now. Something deep down in my soul breaks free. Swallowing, I choke on the emotions that seem to be suffocating me. My brothers don't say a word. They sit with me. They give me support without words or judgment. They have my back. Out of all the moments in my life leading up to this one, this time, it means the most. We pass the bottle around a few more times. Logan and Gabriel call their women to let them know they won't be driving home tonight. Only because they got shit-faced with me while we talked about the past and talked about the plans we are making for our futures.

Every one of mine includes Mila and Ava by my side.

## 26

## MILA

*S tay.* The word was on the tip of my tongue as I watched Reid walk out the door yesterday. I sat paralyzed on the floor unable to fully comprehend what was happening. He said he needed time to think.

On the one hand, I completely understand him wanting to process the revelation we both had discovered together, but on the other hand, I'm terrified of what the outcome will be. What if he can't get past the fact I was with his brother? What if he thinks I'm lying? I hate the unknown.

I stayed on the sofa all night, staring at the door. Waiting for him to come back home. He never did. I finally fell asleep around 2:00 am. When I woke up a little bit ago, after only a couple of hours of sleep, I was disappointed he didn't show. I think that pretty much tells me what I needed to know. Now I almost regret selling the house. The thought of Ava and I having to move out of Reid's place has my stomach in knots. She's become attached to Reid; she won't understand. Twenty-four hours ago, Reid and I were so sure of each other.

The doorbell ringing brings me out of my inner turmoil.

When I open the door, I'm met with my friend, Bella. The moment when her concerned eyes find mine, I allow myself to break down. Bella wraps her arms around me without question and holds me. I don't know how long we go on like this, but when I finally get my emotions under control, I sit down on the sofa and ask, "You know, don't you?"

Squeezing my hand, Bella shakes her head, "I don't know anything. Logan called last night to tell me he was staying at the clubhouse and wouldn't be home. He said something was up with Reid, and he needed his brothers. He mentioned I should come by first thing this morning to check on you but didn't give me any details. Do you want to tell me what happened?"

So, I start from the beginning; I tell her everything. All the way up to Reid walking out last night. Bella sits stunned for a moment before opening her mouth, "This is unbelievable. I know you've mentioned before Ava's father had passed, but Noah...Reid's Noah? Wow," she says, stunned.

"I guess if I had confided in you sooner, than none of this would be happening."

"What do you mean?" she asks with a confused look.

"You've known the club for over a year, and we've been friends for longer. Not once did I tell you about Ava's father aside from the fact he's dead. I didn't know how to tell anyone. It's hard enough with Ava getting older and starting to ask questions I don't have the answers to. I got pregnant from a one-night stand with a guy who I didn't even know his last name or anything about him. What kinds of stuff am I supposed to tell my daughter? She knows her father is in heaven, but what about the other stuff? What was his favorite color? His favorite food? Simple things I should be able to tell her, so she feels like she knows him...has a piece of him. I can't give that to my daughter, so I avoided the subject altogether. It has always been easier. My fear is she will grow up feeling like a piece of her is missing. A year after Ava was born, I went back to that same house where Noah's party was. I went there in hopes of finding his friend so that I could ask questions. I thought, what if Noah had a family? Maybe they would want to know about Ava. But I was too late. I know how stupid it was not to have found out right away, but I had just found out Noah was dead. I was in shock, and then there was everything that happened with my parents when I got home," I finish placing my face in my hands. I had been an idiot, and I had paid for it.

"Mila, listen to me, you are not stupid. You were nineteen and just found out you were pregnant. We all make mistakes. And look at it like this. All those things you couldn't tell Ava before about her father, now you can. Reid is going to be able to tell her all about him. She may not have her father, but she has Reid."

"He didn't come home last night, Bella. Seeing Ava might prove to be too much of a reminder for him. What if he finds he can't be with us?" I question even though I don't expect her to have the answers. Nobody but Reid does, and he's not here.

"You know that's not the kind of man Reid is. He's confused and hurting right now, but I have faith he won't disappoint." Bella says those words as if she's so sure. I don't want Reid to look at my daughter and be reminded of the pain of losing his brother.

After letting Bella's words settle, I decide I'm going to have to accept whatever decision Reid comes to. With each minute he stays gone, it's becoming clear what his decision is. I don't blame him.

"You have this look on your face like you're thinking the worst and are possibly going to do something hastily," Bella notices.

"I'm thinking about what my next move is going to be," I confess. "Reid doesn't want to come home because I'm here. He's too nice of a man to ask me to leave, so I'll make it easy on him."

"What the hell are you going on about, Mila?"

Standing up from the sofa, I walk into the kitchen for some much-needed coffee. "I'm talking about me finding another place to stay. I can get a hotel for a few days until I find an apartment or something," I shrug, trying to act nonchalant, but just saying the words out loud is tearing me up inside.

"Wait a minute," Bella insists, coming up behind me. "You're jumping to conclusions prematurely here, Mila. You don't know that Reid wants you to move out. And I bet anything he doesn't. Both of you need time to absorb this revelation. I know you're in fight or flight mode. Do you love him?"

At Bella's question, I stop what I'm doing and look at her, "Yes, I love Reid."

"Then quit with all this crazy talk about leaving, and fight. Relationships are not easy. Sometimes it will be him that is fighting, and sometimes it will be you. Right now, you both need to fight. Besides the club, Noah was all Reid had. Reid was his big brother; he felt responsible for Noah. Losing him nearly destroyed him. Now Reid's learned not only does his brother have a child—a living, breathing piece of him, but his brother had that child with the woman HE is now in love with. Reid's head is a jumbled mess, but I promise you his heart is with you. Was Reid leaving the right choice? I don't know. But the real question now is—are you going to leave too, or are you going to choose to stay and fight? Let him come back home and see you are still here. That you choose him."

Once again, Bella is right. She always seems to see the logic in moments like this. I immediately began to think the worst and assume Reid is not in this with me. I need to do as Bella suggests. I need to fight to show the man I love. I'm still here. I believe in us and what we have together. I can only hope Reid does too.

After two cups of coffee and my nerves less on edge, I wait.

## 27

## REID

Fuck, my head is killin' me. Drinkin' with my brothers like that is not something I planned on doing. I barely remember making it upstairs last night. It takes a few minutes, but standing under the spray of water helps to clear my brain fog long enough to rewind all the events that lead to the massive hangover I'm sporting. I can't imagine what Mila must have thought when I didn't return home. Finishing my shower, I get dressed in the same clothes, then I walk downstairs to the kitchen, hoping someone may have gotten up before me and made some coffee. As soon as I walk through the door, Prez is standing at the counter in the middle of pouring a mug of coffee for himself.

"Reid. I saw your bike outside. What the hell you doin' here this early?"

Lifting my hand, I run my fingers through my still damp hair and continue my path toward getting coffee. "It's a long fuckin' story, Prez," I inform him, hoping he'll let it be.

"Get you a cup of coffee and have a seat. I got nothin' but time, son," he clarifies as he pulls out a chair at the table.

I should have known he wouldn't let it be. Me being here like this is far from average. It doesn't make it any better walking into the kitchen, looking as rough as I do. After I fix my coffee, I stride over and take a seat across from him at the table and take a decent gulp and wait. Jake stares at me over the rim of his mug before he sets it down and speaks.

"You gonna tell me what's going on, or you gonna make me dig it out of you?"

"Found out Mila's daughter Ava is Noah's," I repeat for the second time in hours. Even for Jake, this is huge. He loved Noah as if he were his own too. A brief look of surprise shadows his face.

"You got my attention. Why don't you start from the beginning with this new-found information," he urges.

He intently listens to me retell how everything went down yesterday and why I'm here this morning. Not once does he interject with questions. He allows me to unload all of it. Talking with Jake comes as easy as it would have if my Pops were sitting across from me instead.

"Sounds like you had one hell of a day. Tell me this. You stop and think about what all this might have meant to Mila? You stop and think about the state you left her in when you hopped on your bike and left her. Left her alone?" he chastises.

I mean. *Fuck.* I needed to process everything. It's not like I was never going to go back home. Too many thoughts were running through my head, and too many emotions were wreaking havoc. Then it dawns on me. I keep saying I or me. Jake is right. I didn't think about her at all. I was only thinking about myself and how I was feeling. I hang my head, worried I might have fucked things up with Mila. How can she trust me to love her when I walked out the door because truth and reality were too much for me to handle at that moment?

"I need to get home," I push my chair from the table and stand.

"You hold on to her, son. She's helped you more than you

realize. We've all seen it. Life is too fuckin' short to try and walk the earth alone," he tells me with a distant look in his eyes.

Leaving my coffee sitting on the table, I turn to walk out of the kitchen. Before I reach the doorway, I hear Jake's chair scratch as it slides on the floor, and I look over my shoulder as he stands and takes a few steps toward me and says one more thing.

"Your old man would be proud. Proud of who you are and the man you have become, Reid. And I couldn't be any prouder myself. Now go get your family, son." Then he pulls me in for a hug.

"Thanks, Jake," I tell him as we part. Leaving him lookin' more tired than usual, I head out into the morning air, mount my bike, and head toward my future. Mila and Ava.

When the firehouse comes into view, I notice Bella's blue mustang sitting on the side of the road. Knowing they will have heard the rumble of the bike's engine; I go ahead and pull up near the steps and park. With each step as I climb the stairs, my heart pounds a little faster. Punching in the code, I unlock the door and turn the knob and step inside to find Mila and Bella sitting on the couch. Mila's red-rimmed and sad eyes gut me. I did this to her. I'm the reason for her tears. I hurt her. Rooted in place, I stare at her beautiful face.

"I'm going to get going. If you need me for anything, you call," Bella hugs her friend, then gets up and gathers her things from the table. Walking right by me, she leaves quietly, closing the door behind her. I don't take it personally. She was here to take care of and support Mila. She left, knowing I need to fix things.

I stride in the direction of Mila. She stands from the couch. I cradle her face in the palm of my hands and tell her, "I am so sorry. I should have never left yesterday," I confess, wanting so badly to kiss her, but I wait. Her lip quivers.

"I understand. It's okay. It's a lot to take in," she replies holding back her emotions. Guarding herself. From me.

I shake my head from side to side, "No, Kitten. What I did—leaving you was not okay. Ava being my brother's daughter, changes nothing. I want **you**. I need **you**. I'm so far in love with you I can't breathe without you," I confess. And it's true. She and her daughter mean everything to me. They became an essential part of my life weeks ago.

Waiting no longer, I bring my lips to hers. I kiss her softly and slowly. I pour my heart into the kiss. She wraps her arms around my neck as our kiss deepens. Not into a hot and heavy kiss, but one of longing, one of need. When we come up for air, her voice isn't but a whisper.

"I was scared. Scared something might have happened to you. Scared you didn't want us. Scared I would never again get to feel your lips on mine. Feel the way my skin tingles when you touch me. I love you, Reid. I didn't know. I'm so sorry I didn't know," she takes a shuddered breath.

I tilt her head back, so I can look into her gorgeous eyes and brush her hair from her face with my fingertips. It's my turn to plead. "I'm so sorry I hurt you. I'm sorry I left you alone when you needed me the most. I will spend the rest of my life making it up to you."

"I love you. Ava and I, we both love you," she tells me.

"I love both of you too. We can and will make this work," I reassure her. Mila looks exhausted. I'm sure she didn't get any rest staying up with worry and doubt. Backing us up, I lower myself to the couch and lean back, guiding her to follow my lead. Doing so, she settles back between my legs with her back resting against my chest. Grabbing the throw from the end of the sofa, I drape it across us, and I rest my arm just under her breast and hold her close to me. "We have a little more time before Ava wakes up. Rest, Kitten. I'm not going anywhere." Linking her fingers with mine she melts into me. She falls asleep, and sometime after, I do the same until I'm woken by a small tickle running down my nose. I open my eyes to find Ava, who has awakened me the same way I've seen her momma wake her so many times before. She is standing beside the couch with her teddy dangling at her side. Smiling at me, she whispers, "Can we make pancakes?"

I can't help but look upon her face in a whole new light. I'm staring into the eyes of my brother. I take in every detail as if I've never seen her before. Her hair is the same color as Noah's. Even her smile is his smile. It tugs at my heart. "Sure, baby girl. You going to help me out?" I smile back at her. She eagerly nods her head. I hate to disturb Mila, but I know getting out from under her will not be graceful, but I slowly do my best. Moaning, Mila stirs and looks up at me. "We have a hungry little girl who's requested pancakes," I look down and tell her.

"Mmm, that sounds good. I'll put on some fresh coffee and start some bacon if you two can handle the rest." She reaches out and catches hold of her daughter then proceeds to tickle her side, causing her to break out in laughter.

Standing at the stove, Mila monitors the bacon sizzling in the skillet while Ava stands on a step stool at my side and helps me flip pancakes on the electric grill nearby. I once thought the club and my career was everything, and I would never want or need more in my life. I was wrong.

---

ONE DAY HAS LED to the next, and before I know it, life has moved on in the most natural way possible. Mila finally signed papers and closed on the house. She was hoping to meet the new owners, but they couldn't attend the meeting in person. We've just about completed the current construction project the company was working on, and in about a week, we will break ground on the resort just outside of town. Despite the fact that Mila has plenty of money at her fingertips, she has decided to keep working. She loves her job at the nursing home, says in some ways it helps with not having her Grams near.

Turns out, sharing memories and pictures of my brother with Ava has by far been the best therapy I could have ever asked for. All this brings us to today. Ava's fifth birthday. We're out here at Gabriel and Alba's place to have the party because our space just won't accommodate everyone. One thing Mila did splurge on was Ava's party since she didn't have the means to do it before. She is throwing her a princess themed party because our little girl is obsessed with princesses and everything girly. A blow-up bounce house that looks like a castle sits in the middle of the backyard. And in the back corner, believe it or not, is a small six horse carousel. Don't ask me who he knew or what he did, but this birthday surprise was from Quinn.

Mila made sure everything was taken care of, right down to a local business catering the food along with Grace agreeing to make the cake. Right now, she and some of the other women are inside putting the finishing touches to all the party favors and getting Ava into her costume while the guys and I are hanging in the backyard waiting for people to start showing up. It seems like family parties and hanging out waiting on our women are slowly becoming a routine for us.

"Too fuckin' pink," Gabriel remarks standing at my right with his arms crossed as he looks out at his transformed backyard.

"Embrace your feminine side, man," Quinn goads him while he places a pink and purple polka dot party hat on top of his head.

Grunting, Gabriel gives his response. "The only feminine side I'll be embracing is when I'm holdin' my woman."

Just about the time Quinn wants to run his mouth some more, we hear several car doors slamming. Over the next twenty minutes, family and friends start to arrive, including River and his daughter. After he sets his daughter free to play with some of the other kids, I signal for him to walk over.

"Brothers, this is River. He helped with the whole shit show that went down with Mila's parents," I introduce them. Firm handshakes get passed around.

"It's nice to meet you guys."

"Why don't you join the rest of us for a beer?" I gesture to him.

"That would be great," he replies.

We all end up shootin' the shit while we wait. River happens to be a cool guy. I've even asked his advice on a few legal aspects concerning some new contracts we were looking at, and so far, his knowledge seems to have worked in my favor.

Before the women come out with the birthday girl and get all the party games underway, I decide to engage the guys in some more serious talk. Rubbing the back of my neck, I speak, "Listen, Mila has a fancy black-tie charity event coming up in a few weeks. This, of course, is at the same time we have the charity run scheduled. I'm wondering if you guys can help me pull something off."

Collectively they nod their heads in agreement.

"Whatever you need, we'll make it happen, brother. What do you have in mind?" Prez says, eager to find out more. Before I can go into any further detail, the women make their entrance with the birthday girl front and center dressed as Cinderella.

"Mind if we resume this chat sometime tomorrow at the clubhouse?" I ask them all.

"We'll be there," Logan says.

Weaving my way through a crowd of children who have gathered to plunder their tiny grabby hands into the large bucket Bella and Sofia are holding loaded down with noisemakers and candy, I reach down and scoop Ava up into my arms. "You're beautiful, baby girl." I smile at her.

Giggling, she fusses with her dress, "Thank you," she replies.

After tickling her, I kiss the top of her head and put her down. Grabbing some toys of her own, she joins her friends making a beeline toward Quinn who has already started up the carousel ride for the kids.

My gaze lands on Mila, who is standing across the yard, talking to Alba. Turning her head in my direction, she looks directly at me and smiles. It's at this moment I feel something I haven't felt in a long time. I feel complete.

# MILA

"What about this one, Mila?" Looking up from the rack at our favorite vintage boutique, I eye the dress Bella is holding. The hospital charity event is tonight, and I waited until the last minute to shop for a dress, so I called Bella in a panic this morning and asked for her help. Thirty minutes later, she and Alba were at my door. Alba is ready to pop any day and opted to sit this shopping trip out. I don't blame her. My friends are lifesavers.

"Omg! I love that one. What size is it?" I asked, walking up to her.

Bella peeks at the tag, "Your size," she answers.

Stepping out of the dressing room with the dress on, Bella's huge smile tells me all I need to know.

Turning to face the mirror, I stare at my reflection. It's perfect. The dress is black satin, floor-length with an open back. The material of the dress feels cold against my warm skin. The way it clings to my body makes it feel as if I'm wearing nothing.

"Mila, you look stunning," Bella gushes. "You have to get this one."

Running my hands down my sides over the silky material, I

turn to peer over my left shoulder and study my reflection in the mirrored wall. "This is the one," I confess.

Back at mine and Reid's place, I'm sitting on a stool in the bathroom while Alba does my hair, and Bella applies my makeup while Gabe and Ava play together on the bedroom floor. Could I have done all this myself? Yes, but the duo decided they needed to make a fuss over me.

Reid left yesterday with the club on a charity run they had planned months ago, so, unfortunately, he's unable to attend the event with me tonight. I told him it was no big deal, but he still feels lousy about not going. Honestly, I'm a little disappointed to be going stag, but I understand the run is equally as important. I would never come between him and his obligations to his club.

Gazing at our reflections in the mirror, Alba pauses from curling my hair as she places her hand on her back and stretches.

"Are you alright?" I ask with concern. I've noticed her do this several times in the past hour.

"Yeah, I'm okay. My back is a little achy is all. I promise I'm fine," Alba insists.

"Here, I'll finish her hair. You go sit down for a little bit," Bella intervenes, taking the curling iron from her sister's hands. Alba rolls her eyes but does as she's told. I love their relationship. I'm sometimes envious of it. I always wanted siblings growing up.

I look forward to the day I can give Ava a brother or sister. With her turning five, I've come to realize I don't want there to be a significant age gap between her and her siblings. I want them to grow up together, but how do I even bring up the subject with Reid? I don't want to rush anything. It's just lately I find myself thinking more and more about having a family with Reid.

"What are you thinking about?" Bella asks. "You look deep in thought."

Letting out a sigh, I answer her, "I was thinking about how I'd like to have more kids," I confess.

"Have you and Reid been talking about it?"

"No. I haven't brought the subject up. We've finally gotten into a comfortable place since all the craziness that has happened. I don't want to rock the boat. That and it's too soon to be talking about kids." I wave my hand at her, "You know, it's probably my crazy hormones, and I'm around Alba all the time. Baby fever is rubbing off on me, I suppose." I decide to steer the conversation in Bella's direction, "Are you and Logan still trying?" I watch as something passes over her face. A smile just as quickly appears.

"Still trying, but we are having a hell of a good time trying." Swiftly changing the subject, she announces that she is finished.

"Holy shit!" I blurt out once I get a look at myself. My hair hangs in loose curls down my back. The smoky shadow Bella applied makes my eye color pop. To top it all off, she painted my lips with crimson red lipstick. "You two have worked some serious magic." I stand in awe, gawking at my reflection. Looking at my watch, I realize I only have an hour to get dressed and to the event. "Shit! I have to hurry." Walking over to the closet where my gown is hanging on the hook, I strip out of my clothes and carefully remove it from the hanger, letting the slinky material float down over my body. Stepping into a pair of black heels, I wrap lace ties around my ankles adding five inches to my height.

"Stand there for one second, I want to get a picture," Bella insists.

After she has taken several snaps, I give myself one more glance in the mirror before walking over to the dresser and grabbing my clutch.

"Momma, you look like a pwinces."

Leaning down, I kiss Ava on her cheek. "Thanks, baby girl. You be good, and momma will see you later." I turn my attention back to Bella and Alba, "Thank you for everything," I say, hugging them.

"You're welcome, now go before you're late," Alba ushers.

I arrive at Dr. Walker's home, where the event is taking place.

Parking in the circular drive, I step out of my car, and the valet instantly greets me. Placing my ticket in my clutch, I make my way around the side of the house, where I see a large white canopy. Underneath the tent is an array of round tables with white linen tablecloths along with white chairs that have been spaced evenly throughout the area. Located in the very front is a podium. I feel my anxieties start to grow. I realize I will soon be standing at the podium giving a speech to roughly two hundred people.

A woman stands at the entrance of the tent and speaks as I walk up, "Name?" she asks.

"Mila Vaughn."

"You're seated at table one. Dinner will be delivered to your table at 7:00 pm. Followed by the announcement of the winners for the silent auction, which is taking place right over there." She points to the right where several sets of large tables are lined around the inside perimeter of another tent. "Then you'll be called up on stage to give your speech, Ms. Vaughn. Any questions?" she finishes.

"No, I think I got it. Thank you," I politely tell her before walking in.

When I get to my table, I notice I'll be sitting with the director of the hospital, Dr. Walker and his wife, Claire.

"Good evening, Mila," he greets me with a warm smile. "You look lovely."

I don't miss the ugly sneer Claire gives me. I take my seat. "Thank you, Dr. Walker."

"Please call me Liam. I'm pleased you decided to give this year's speech. I'd also like to offer my condolences on your grandmother's passing."

"Thank you," I reply, trying not to choke on my emotions at the mention of Grams.

"I see you came alone, Mila," Claire leans into my personal space and murmurs. The comment hits the target nerve she was after. I shouldn't let her get to me. Usually, I wouldn't, but I do wish Reid could have been here. Tonight, however, not being about her or myself, I squash the idea of shoving her face into the appetizers sitting in front of her.

Instead, I excuse myself and walk over to the tent and tables they have set up and check out the various auction items. Amongst the items is an all-inclusive trip to the Four Seasons Resort Maldives at Landaa Giraavaru. I flip through the color catalog they have placed on the display. I've never been outside of New York or Montana unless you count the states I passed over on my way back and forth during my summer trips as a kid. The thought alone of enjoying a vacation like this, getting to lay around in the warmth of the sun. The green-blue waters are so vivid and alive with colorful sea creatures—I retrieve a bid sheet from the table. Every stroke of my pen as it writes out my bid fills me with excitement. Even if I don't win the trip, I will write a check for the same amount before I leave tonight to donate in my Grams honor. Afterward, I wander back to my table just as dinner is about to be served. From the options given, I settle on the roasted Cornish hen with rosemary buttered fingerling potatoes and bacon wrapped asparagus bundles. Aside from sharing brief moments of conversation with other contributors seated at my table, I'm able to finish half my meal before the event coordinator starts announcing the winners of the auctioned items. When she gets to the exotic island vacation, I bid on. I hold my breath.

"The winning bid for a gorgeous all-inclusive vacation at the Four Seasons Resort Maldives at Landaa Giraavaru," she pauses as she gets handed a piece of paper, "Mila Vaughn. It seems this was a highly sought-after item tonight. Congratulations."

I can't help the smile that overtakes my face.

"You? How in the world can you afford a bid that size, and it had to have been a large sum to outbid me. How can you afford such a thing on a nurse's salary?" Claire looks down her nose with a smug disgusted look on her Botox'd face.

"Claire, that's enough," her husband Liam scolds his wife in front of the entire table. Opening and closing her mouth, she shoots a knife-cutting glare my way before standing up and walking away from the table in the direction of their home.

"Mila, my apologies for my wife's behavior tonight," Liam tells me. I didn't miss the underlying tone of detest when he said "wife".

"I appreciate the apology." I'm about to say more when the lady on stage announces, "Ladies and Gentlemen, our speaker for the evening is a nurse—a caregiver herself. Who better to stand up here at this podium. Please welcome Ms. Mila Vaughn."

Standing, I smooth down my dress. Applause fills the night air, giving me the courage to put one heel in front of the other. Afraid I might mess up and forget something, I retrieve my notes I had stashed in my clutch. Exhaling the warm night air, I start to speak.

"Good evening. I'm honored to speak here tonight." I wet my lower lip, look down at my notes, then lift my eyes to the 200 plus guests in the crowd. "Alzheimer's is the sixth-leading cause of death in the United States. I can also tell you almost two-thirds of Americans with Alzheimer's are women. One of those women happened to be my grandmother, Charlotte Scott. I cared for her for a long time, doing everything I possibly could before the disease started to progress to the point she needed more care than I could provide for her at home. You see, I'm what society describes as a 'sandwich generation' caregiver—meaning I cared not only for an aging grandparent but also for a child, my daughter who just turned 5. At times, more times than I can count, I would feel overwhelmed and brokenhearted. What a lot of people fail to understand is Alzheimer's takes a devastating toll on not only the person having to live with the debilitating disease, but it affects the caregivers and families as well. Watching a loved one lose pieces of themselves, like forgetting the person they fell in love with or reliving a sad moment in life repeatedly because they got stuck in the past—because they became so lost in the present."

I pause to collect myself and swallow past my emotions. "Watching them stop right in the middle of eating a meal because they become confused with the simple task of how to use a fork to feed themselves." The memory of Grams at Christmas dinner last year grips at my heart.

Scanning the sea of faces, I continue, "I urge you to open your hearts and of course, your wallets. The donations given tonight will not only benefit the research and ongoing advancements in finding a cure for Alzheimer's, but it will also help families cover the many out of pocket expenses associated with caring for their loved ones and provide much-needed counseling for the patient and the family members affected."

A distant roar—like a million horses running on open pastures starts to echo through the night sky. As the sound amplifies, you can feel the vibrations from the rumble course through your body. In the distance, a massive sea of lights heads our direction. I stand rooted to my spot while men and women stand to look on as dozens of motorcycles travel down the long private driveway of Dr. Walker's home. I don't have to make him out. I know he's in the formation somewhere. One lone biker weaves his way through parked limos and high dollar vehicles, eventually coming to a slow stop at the edge of the white tent. I stand frozen until my eyes connect with Reid's. This man is every bit the definition of handsome. Dressed in a black, well-tailored tux, he dismounts his bike.

*Be still my heart.*

Standing at his full height, Reid doesn't say a word. His eyes tell me everything. He's here for me; all of them are here for me.

Giving me his signature smirk, Reid encourages me to continue. I clear my throat to gain the crowd's attention.

"I apologize for the noise, ladies, and gentlemen, but my family likes to be fashionably late. I'm going to try and end my speech on a more positive note. There is good among the bad. Those good days—maybe even brief moments of clarity your loved one will experience; hold onto them. Moments when they know; they are aware they have found their way out of the dark. Cling to that, latch on to each other because time is precious. It's those memories I hold on to. It's those moments I will share with my daughter. Charlotte Scott inspired me to become a nurse. Giving and taking care of people was not only in her nature, but it's also what she was put on this earth to do. To spread compassion and give her love to those around her. She instilled all those core values in me. I'm standing up here for my grandmother...I'm her voice." I flip the page to wrap up my speech.

Absently, I continue reading the printed words. "Finding Solace," I seek Reid out after reading two words I know are not my own. Placing his finger on his lips to suppress a smile, he nods his head, wanting me to continue. I feel my knees wobble. Dropping my eyes, I read aloud again, "Your touch was my waking. Your kiss my oxygen—the air I breathe. In you, I see thousands of memories we have yet to make."

Overwhelmed, my voice trails off.

I close my eyes.

I get lost in the words—his words.

I didn't realize he was now standing right next to me. His scent invades my lungs and consumes all my senses. His love radiates off of him; It blankets me like the warm summer sun.

"Look at me, Kitten," his warm breath floats across my ear as he leans in.

Lifting my head, I open my eyes. The only sound being the soft whispers of the wind. When I look out in the crowd, I spot all the guys standing toward the back. Along with the rest of the family—my family. And holding my little girl is Bella.

I smile.

Grabbing my trembling hands, Reid tells me, "I made a promise a while back to one very remarkable lady. I promised her I would watch every sunset with you. I plan on keeping my promise. You fixed all my broken pieces, Mila; you and Ava. Let me make up for all the moments I should have been kissing you. Marry me?" he asks me.

I don't make him wait. "You've got a lot of making up to do." I smile, and he kisses me.

# EPILOGUE

## Mila

Finding a quiet moment to myself, I gaze out at the lake as the sun begins to set. As the vibrant colors of oranges and yellows start to paint the surface of the water, I think about Grams. This is the time of day I feel her with me the most.

When Reid and I decided to marry right away, I knew as we promised the rest of our lives to one another, I wanted it to be at the exact moment the sun-kissed the earth. After hearing of mine and Reid's plan to marry, Bella quickly offered up her and Logan's place on the lake. The whole club, our family, has pitched in to make today a day we will never forget. Bella has indeed been my rock since we have known each other, and I can honestly say there is no better friend than her.

I look at myself in the full-length mirror and smooth down my dress. My something old is the same wedding dress my grandmother wore when she married my grandfather in 1952. It's a long sleeve, ivory lace gown. The only alterations I had done to it were opening the backside to expose my back, making it more modern and a little sexy. Everything else about it was perfect. My hair is pinned up on one side with a mass of curls sweeping down over my right shoulder, keeping my makeup simple with a pop of red painted on my lips.

For something borrowed, a stunning piece of antique jewelry I have attached to my bouquet that Bella found on the trip to the Bahamas Logan took her on months ago. My something blue comes from Alba; a pair of small sapphire earrings and finally, something new. As I was getting ready earlier, Ava came in with a little blue box. I opened it and nestled inside was a delicate silver chain attached to a small infinity symbol. The note tucked underneath it merely read, *I love you, Kitten.*

Turning to my left, I look at my maid of honor, Bella, as she hands me my bouquet. "You look beautiful, Mila," she says, beaming, then she pulls me in for a hug.

"Ready, Momma?" Ava's cheerful voice asks, stealing my attention.

Looking down at my daughter, I smile. I take in how beautiful she looks in her dress. The top is sleeveless and ivory in color, while the bottom fades into a blush pink tulle that reaches the tips of her toes covered in pink ballet flats. Her bouncy blonde curls are swept up in a high ponytail, topped off with light pink roses. Ava was very much involved in the planning of our wedding, and she insisted on pink, so the flowers and her dress were all for her. She is also walking me down the aisle today.

"Let's do it, baby girl." I smile, giving her a wink.

. . .

ONCE BELLA MAKES her way down the aisle, everyone stands from their seats. As music fills the air, Ava places her tiny hand in mine, and we make our way toward our future.

"Who gives this pretty lady away?" Quinn grins, directing his question toward Ava.

"Me," Ava announces with a giggle while swishing her tulle dress back and forth. Before Ava lets go of my hand to walk toward Bella, Reid clears his throat.

"I have something I want to say to Ava first," Reid announces. Kneeling, he takes her small hands in his. My heart swells. Overwhelmed with emotions, my eyes well up with tears as I watch and listen.

"Ava, my sweet girl. I'm so honored to have you in my life. I promise to always hold your hand. I promise to always show you how a man should treat a woman by the way I love your Momma. Above all else, I promise to always protect you and take care of you."

By the time he finishes with his vows, Ava leaps into his arms. The depth of connection the two of them have with each other is undeniable. He ushers her over toward Bella before standing and wiping the tears from my cheeks with his thumbs.

"You ready?" He smiles.

Taking a breath, I recite my vows, "Reid, you showed us our hearts were missing someone...you." I smile at him. "In you, I have found a new beginning. You are everything I have always hoped for and more. You give me strength and courage every day. You've given me a family I've never had." I pause long enough to look out at the sea of faces standing with us today, then look back at Reid. "You've given me a home. You are our home. I love you." I blink, and another set of tears trail down my face.

Taking my face in his hands, Reid leans in as if to kiss me. "You chose me. It was you who made me feel worthy of being loved. It was you who had all the strength, and you gave it to me when I needed it the most. You breathed life back into me. Mila, you and Ava are my home. You're mine, Kitten. I will forever love you." His lips crash down on mine. Cheers erupt.

"Fuck, Yeah!" Quinn boasts before announcing, "I give you Mr. And Mrs. Reid Carter, motherfuckers!"

# REID

When we make it to the clubhouse, the party is in full force. Family, food, laughter, and my beautiful as fuck wife surround me, and I couldn't be happier than I am right now.

The sight of Mila and Ava walking down the aisle toward me almost brought me to my damn knees. I have Mila to thank for bringing me solace. My soul finally feels at peace. Every time I look at Ava, I see Noah. I still can't believe I have a living, breathing piece of him in my life. I vow to live each day fulfilling the promise I made to him.

A few weeks ago, Mila and I sat down with Ava and explained to her Noah was her father and my brother. Being the amazing little person she is, Ava took it all in stride. She had questions that we answered along with showing her pictures of him. Photos that are now proudly displayed around our home. It was the question Ava asked later the same day that had me ready to rip my heart out and hand it to her as we were sitting down to eat dinner.

"Reid, can you be my Daddy?"

I cut my eyes over to Mila, who had tears streaming down her face. Choking past my own emotions, I turned back toward Ava. "Is that what you want, sweetheart?"

She had nodded her head vigorously, making her curls bounce when she answered me, "I want you to be my Daddy."

I knew this little girl would own my heart forever.

Jake raps his knuckles, brings my attention back to the present. Lifting his chin, he gives me the signal I've been waiting on. Standing up, I stride across the room with my sights set on my bride who is talking to Bella and Alba.

Wrapping my arms around her middle, and I bury my face in her neck, breathing in her scent.

"Go get changed and come take a ride with me," I murmur and smile when I feel her body shudder. I swat her ass. "Go. I'll be outside waiting for you."

Fifteen minutes later, Mila is on the back of my bike, and I am making the turn down the street where her grandmother's house is. I feel the moment she realizes the direction we are heading toward because her arms squeeze tighter around me. She hasn't been back to the house since moving out. The club has been keeping a secret from her, and it's time for her to find out what that secret is. Pulling into the driveway, I park my bike next to Jake's, where he and Sofia are standing. I cut the engine while Mila climbs off the back. Taking her helmet off, I take in the shocked expression on her face.

"What's going on?" she questions me with confusion.

"I'll let Sofia explain it all to you, Kitten." I take her hand in mine, and we make our way toward Jake and Sofia. I watch Sofia smile at Mila, then take her by the hand and lead her toward the front door. Jake and I follow. A gasp leaves Mila's lips as Sofia stops her in front of a wooden sign hanging to the right of the front door just under the porch light, which reads *New Hope House, The Charlotte Scott Foundation.*

"The club, well, Jake bought the house, and after all the

paperwork and licensing goes through, your grandmother's home will become a safe house for women and their children who need to start a new life," Sofia explains to her.

"I don't know what to say," Mila breathes.

I walk up behind her and embrace her in my arms. "Your Grams will continue to help others. They will feel the safety and love held within these walls just as you did," I whisper in her ear.

Breaking away from me, she hugs Sofia before walking over to Jake and thanking him. "Thank you."

"You take care of him, and that's all the thanks I need," I hear him tell her.

Turning her head, she makes eye contact with me. "Forever."